Jour[...] the Half-Door

RUSTY WATSON

Library of Congress Cataloging-in-Publication Data

Names: Watson, Rusty, author.
Title: Journey through the half-door / Rusty Watson.
Description: Albuquerque, NM : Casa de Snapdragon LLC, [2016]
Identifiers: LCCN 2016042766 (print) | LCCN 2016049288 (ebook) |
ISBN
   9781937240752 (pbk.) | ISBN 9781937240769 (epub)
Subjects: | GSAFD: Love stories
Classification: LCC PS3623.A8735 J68 2016 (print) | LCC
PS3623.A8735 (ebook)
   | DDC 813/.6--dc23
LC record available at https://lccn.loc.gov/2016042766

20161019

Casa de Snapdragon LLC
12901 Bryce Avenue, NE
Albuquerque, NM 87112
casadesnapdragon.com

Printed in the United States of America

For Margarette, my grandmother, a woman of Faith

1896 – 1967

and

Kay Judah, historic fashion instructor, Washington University

The Tapestry Poem
Corrie Ten Boom

My Life is but a weaving
Between my God and me.
I cannot choose the colors
He weaveth steadily.
Oft' times He weaveth sorrow;
And I in foolish pride
Forget He sees the upper
And I the underside.
Not 'til the loom is silent
And the shuttles cease to fly
Will God unroll the canvas
And reveal the reason why.
The dark threads are as needful
In the weaver's skillful hand
As the threads of gold and silver
In the pattern He has planned
He knows, He loves, He cares;
Nothing this truth can dim.
He gives the very best to those
Who leave the choice to Him.
Life is But a Weaving.

May the blessing of light be on you; light without and light within.
May the blessed sunlight shine on you and warm your heart till it
glows like a great peat fire.

    —Irish Blessing for Brighter Days

Contents

Foreword

Every family has a poignant story to share. Each soul on Earth has obtained a past that stretches into the present. However, our life is not uniquely ours to claim. Perhaps we should consider our lives merely a continuation of our ancestors' struggle to persevere in the world, as they knew it.

For example, I glance around my own home and perched atop my kitchen cabinets are cherished antique objects passed down from my Grandmother and Irish Great-Grandmother. The 1920s glass butter churn, with the sturdy wooden blades, rubbed dark from turning, sits high upon my shelf used only as a decoration. The square black tin container, battered and dented, with rubbed-off gold lettering, once safely harbored spices and flavorings destined for cakes and pies. It rests in the corner of my countertop, and now stands empty for want of a cook who has time to fill it rather than busy writing novels.

These baking and cookware objects were used daily. When I gaze upon them, I wonder if my love of cooking migrated from my Grandmother to me. It seems as if these items continue to beg those of us living in the present to view them worthy and whole once again.

Observing the antiques, I recall as a child, the stories told around the family dining room table and the lessons learned from the buzzing of words and rollicking laughter, while dunking doughnuts in sweetened coffee.

Would it not be honorable to occasionally take down these ancient stories, dust them off, and view them within the context of our own lives? We must learn from the mistakes and fortunes of the past generations in order to proceed with the present and valiantly march into our future.

Journey Through the Half-Door is a story based on my Great-grandmother Dehlias' life, who fled the hardships of Ireland in 1884 and immigrated to America, the "land of opportunity." Oral history has informed me that Dehlia was a woman of grit and determination. Written history and careful research has allowed me to tell her story within the political temperature of the time.

I believe the story of Dehlia resonates with the struggles of many families during immigration, whether coming to America from Ireland or other points of the globe. They may have come to escape repression of gender, to seek freedom from religious persecution, or simply hoping for a better life. The individual facts may be different but the human battle is all very much the same.

Similar to those ancient relics sitting upon our shelves, every once in a while, we need to stop the business of our daily lives and pause to discern where we have come from. Our forgotten heritage needs to be taken down, re-examined, re-considered for its' worth and re- valued again.

After all, sometime in the future, wouldn't your own life merit some small consideration? Then let us move forward, inspecting the treasures of the past to remind us where we come from, what we have become, and what we will always "be."

I hope you enjoy reading *Journey Through the Half-Door* as much as I have enjoyed committing the story to paper!

An Irish Blessing

"May God grant you always...

A sunbeam to warm you,

a moonbeam to charm you,

a sheltering Angel so nothing can harm you,

Laughter to cheer you.

Faithful friends near you.

And whenever you pray, Heaven to hear you."

Go n-e'ire an bo'thar leat! Have a good journey!

Rusty Watson

Chapter One

The Threads That Bind Us

"Mother, Mother, come quickly!" Dorothy Jane shouted over her shoulder. "Nana's crawling onto the windowsill again and I can't convince her to come back inside!" Dorothy's mother, Margarette, bounded up the stairs as fast as she could, untying her freshly laundered apron as she ran. She knew from experience that she might have to laboriously climb out onto the gritty roof to coax her tiny Irish mother back down to safety. Margarette did not want to get her favorite article of clothing dirty, yet again.

"Come on Dear One," Margarette cooed softly to her mother Dehlia, "come down from the ledge and back inside where you will be safe and sound."

"No, no, NO!" Dehlia cried, "I best hurry home before it gets dark! My *Ma'thair* will be vexed if I am not there to help her get dinner on the table before Da gets in from tending the sheep!"

"Nana, this is America, not Ireland and it's the year 1942, not 1878!" Dorothy exclaimed. "How are we ever going to convince you of the here and now?"

Dehlia stopped groping the rough gray shingles of the roof and turned around to look blankly at her granddaughter.

Who is this dark-haired beauty yelling at me and why does she not want me to reach home before Da disowns me? Dehlia thought to herself.

Doesn't she know that times are harsh in County Mayo, with too many hungry mouths to feed and not enough money to go around? *Arrah*, my parents would toss me out of the house for being so insolent! Looking around at her daughter and granddaughter with moist eyes, glazed and lost, Dehlia sadly implored, "Don't you see I need to return home quickly?"

The old woman's mind was filled with the thought of the familiar cottage located in the town of Ballyhaunas, Ireland, nestled snuggly in the heart of the province of Connaught.

"I have much to do before tomorrow!" Dehlia muttered in explanation.

"Tomorrow will be February 1st and St. Brigid's Day, when all the people in our town celebrate the first day of spring. Aye! Glorious springtime in the County of Cork!" Ireland had always been an enchanted land where myth and reality existed side-by-side.

Dehlia followed that delicate thread of thought in her mind's eye as she visualized a beautiful patchwork of green and yellow fields of wheat and rye interspersed with slubs of thatched stone cottages.

Unknown to her, Dehlia did not know then the tangled threads and stubborn knots beginning to form on the back of her life's quilt would lead her far away from home and the familiar traditions that had once grounded her as a young girl.

Growing up in Ireland after the Great Famine, or *"An Ghorta Mho'ir,"* as they say in Gaelic, even thirty years after the invisible fungus spores first devastated the crops, had become a tedious struggle for the Irish population. The blight of 1847 forever changed Irish culture and customs.

Dehlia knitted her eyebrows together and frowned in contemplation as she tried to remember the circumstances that led to her leaving home and forsaking the boy she had loved and cherished with all her heart.

"Ah yes." Dehlia tapped her forehead in recollection and fondly recalled, "My proud *A'thair* was a man of time-worn traditions, who thatched his roof with golden wheat harvested from his own fields. Da would plough the land in the spring and sow it with rye, harrowing it in the old way, with his donkey. When the wheat was luscious and ripe he would cut it with a scythe and re-thatch the roof by means of willow rods. He toiled for weeks in order to make our home warm and snug during the icy winter months. Da was clever and used the local building materials he found among the landscape; white stone for the low foundation walls, smooth timbers from the bogs, and of course, coarse straw from the fields to peg the thatch to the cottage walls.

Some farmers still brought their cattle and pigs into their houses at night. They thought it unlucky if their animals were not able to get a glimpse of the fire in the hearth. It was generally known that cows made more milk if warm and cozy!

Although Da didn't believe in it, others swore that the power of fire dispelled evil spirits. Many of the one-room cabins, which we called a home, were constructed as lean-tos against an old ditch but all proudly sporting an ample fireplace. The Irish have a saying, "You can't cross a ditch or you'll fall down a chimney!"

I see it all now! Dehlia fondly remembered, despite all the cobwebs tangled in her old mind. She had a fine home of three whole rooms with enough warmth and love to surround her parents and enable them to nurture six children. It was the year of Our Lord, 1878.

"*Go meadai Dia thu*! May God make you prosperous!" Margaret Bridget Greely Fleming called out to her man, Thomas, leaning her roughened elbows on the half-door of our cottage and watching as he walked down the path that would take him to his fields and livestock for the day. Margaret loved her half-door because it served to let the light in and keep out unwanted animals. She would often laugh and say, "A woman standing at an open door is wasting time, but leaning on the half-door is just passing time!"

"*Ma' thair*? Can I make a "*brideog*" now to begin our celebration of St. Brigid's Day? Dehlia enthusiastically sang out as she ran through the bottom half of the wooden door. "I just can't wait to make my spud doll!"

"*Nil*," my mother responded. "Don't you know that everyone in this house has daily chores to get through before we celebrate? Why, St. Brigid is the patroness of cattle and dairy and surely her spirit would be vexed if the livestock she were blessing had swollen udders! Now go fetch your eldest sister Annie and the rest of your brothers to help you with the chores. While you're at it, convince your mopey sister Mary to stop cuddling the lambs and contribute as well! After the work is all finished you can fashion your little potato doll out of sticks and rags! Now scat, little one, be quick about you!"

As I begrudgingly ran off to collect my siblings for chores, I was determined to be patient. I happily thought about the two shiny black buttons Annie had gleaned from the bottom of her sewing basket and how I was going to use them for my doll's eyes. I had been spoiled with many indulgences but I was also used to waiting.

In 1878, I was a mere slip of a girl, eleven years old and the youngest of a brood of hardy and hale children born to Margaret and Thomas Fleming. Just as in my birth order, I was used to being last in line, waiting to sidle up to the table to eat dinner, waiting to take my turn at a weekly bath in the family's wooden tub, and of course, waiting to have childish fun until after the daily labors were over.

As I ran, I called out loudly to my oldest sister, Annie, a spinster already at age 21, and also Austin, Mary, Michael and Tom, ages 19, 17, 15 and 13, to hurry and finish their chores so I could begin fashioning my doll. I found Annie busy packing and preparing to leave our home.

"Oh Annie," I cried out, shocked to see her normal happy face so rigid. "What are you doing with your things? Are you packing up your treasures and leaving us?"

"Aye, I am!" she declared. "I'll not waste my life toiling away in this God-forsaken country, waiting for a grubby man to take me as his wife!" she stammered. "Why, I have never been as embarrassed as I was in March, on Shrove Tuesday, when the townspeople sprinkled salt all over me to preserve me hale and hearty until the next year when they could season me again! They all had a good, stout laugh at my expense! Once again, I have been overlooked and not asked to marry so I must take bold action! I'm striking out for a new future, free from prejudices and petty superstitions. I'm leaving Ireland to cross the Atlantic Ocean to America, to make my own fortune in the land of opportunity!" Annie bravely stated.

"Annie, if you sail across that wide ocean away from us we will never see you again!" I wailed with despair as I watched her wad one ragged article of clothing after another into balls and angrily stuff them deep down in her basket.

"Oh I know how you feel, little one, but this is my chance to escape the drudgery of working my life away on this dirty scrap of land! I will be able to turn my back on all the pointed noses that assume I will never wed."

"But Annie, won't you be afraid to take a long ocean voyage? Aren't you scared of what might happen to you in a foreign land? You'll be too far for Da and Mam to watch over you!"

"Well, taking a chance of setting up a life in America is certainly the lesser of the two evils! Who knows? Perhaps luck will be with me and I'll meet a kind, handsome man in the United States. If God is willing, we might even have a bonny family of wee ones."

"Will you write to me? You know I will miss you!" I tearfully sobbed.

"*Mo chuisle*, my darling, not only will I write often and describe ALL the wondrous landmarks I see, I shall promise

Brigid, called to journey forth into the wolf's lair. As long as we both remember to craft the cross and believe that goodness will follow, then you, as well as I, will be safe from harm."

"Oh Annie! I will remember! Just promise to Saint Bridgid that someday you will send for me! Pledge that to me Annie!" I sobbed, fresh tears soaking the front of my bodice.

"I will promise Sweetheart!" Annie agreed. "And until we meet again, all of you, Mam, Da, Mary, Austin, Michael, you and our sweet little Tom, say the table grace of Brigid's monastery each evening to remind us of our home."

"You mean the prayer that goes like this?" I proudly stated, for I knew it by heart. With Annie's encouragement, I timidly began my recitation but gained tenacity as I continued.

[2]I should welcome the poor to my feast,
For they are God's children.
I should welcome the sick to my feast,
For they are God's joy.
Let the poor sit with Jesus at the highest place,
And the sick dance with the angels.
God bless the poor.
God bless the sick,
And bless our human race.
God bless our food,
God bless our drink,
All homes, O God, embrace.

---

[2] Cahill, page 174-75

"Yes child, you have it right. Always remember to be kind to others like Saint Brigid. Extend to them the love we feel for each other in this household. It will keep your thoughts tender and your heart warm on many a cold night."

And so, my beloved sister courageously packed up her lowly kit and embarked on her journey, becoming a beacon of light and a small part of the big Irish diaspora scattering throughout the world.

After Annie departed, I looked around me and seriously doubted if daily life for the human race would ever be easy in our impoverished Ireland. I attributed most of the blame on the consequences of the potato famine from thirty years ago. We Irish have a saying, "seeing is believing but feeling is the God's own truth," and I witnessed the devastation and havoc that the hoary tentacles of famine wove among our younger generation. The debilitating blight had become one with the soil but it also loomed over us, poisoning our very souls. Later on, one astute Irish historian wrote: "The Famine was a crisis of the mind as well as the body."[3]

Although the Famine had certainly wrecked destruction across the land, my Da believed the lack of resources for the Irish workingman was the foundation our rebellion was loosely basted. Despair and starvation fastened the two firmly together and began to suck the hope out of all the mired souls. Over time, in ever tighter and smaller stitches, insidious thoughts began to lurk and weave their murderous ways across our nation's landscape.

------

[3] *In Search of Ancient Ireland*, page 52

Chapter Two

The Great Hunger

Ever the eager student, Dehlia studiously gleaned from her history books, at the National School where she attended, unchallenged knowledge about the insidious root of the Irish struggle. It all began when the potato tuber was brought in 1570 by Sir Walter Raleigh from the New World[4].

The potato had not been native to Ireland but was indeed, welcomed as heaven-sent. It quickly became a cash crop, easy to grow and producing a high yield per acre. The "lumpers", as the farmers were apt to call them, thrived in the damp Irish climate and as a result, the people thrived as well. The Irish population exploded in the period of ease between 1780 and 1847. Dehlias' textbook emphasized potatoes were a staple at every meal and a burly man could often consume as many as fifteen at a single meal!

Awed and amazed, Dehlia asked her father at one evening meal, "How many potatoes could you eat each day when you were a lad?" absolutely sure her Da could have downed at least half as many as that!

"Why, I could eat three meals of potatoes a day and lick

---

[4] *eyewitnesstohistory.com*

my plate clean, especially when my Mam would add milk to the meal! Look at how brawny and sharp I've become!" he bragged as he merrily tapped the tip of Dehlias' freckled nose. Dehlia giggled, for she had to admit, her Da was indeed a very handsome and witty man!

Never satisfied with a simple answer, she asked, "But tell me again how that nasty fungus came to claim our soil and how it rotted our potatoes." Dehlia entreated. "I like to hear you tell the tale, Da. It makes more sense to me when you describe how it challenged our land and its' people."

Da sighed and began to patiently explain, again, that with the increase in numerous Irish sons, the family farms were divided and sub-divided over and over to enable all heirs a small parcel of land in which to farm their crops. As a result of the multiple divisions, individual farmsteads became smaller and unable to sustain a growing family. While it was fortunate that the Irish were fertile with children, it was a thorny problem for the over-worked and divided plots of soil. In the unlucky month of September 1845, an airborne killer fungus, later on called *Phytophthora infestans,* greedily survived among the cargo holds of foreign ships from France, England and a host of other formally stricken nations, stealthily lighting the fuse that sparked a terrible blight.

"I saw for myself how the green stalks and ridges of the potato leaves became wilted and within a very short time the rotting crop of our livelihood was producing a terrible stench in the fields." he mumbled, almost to himself. "It was the stink of death, for sure!"

He continued talking, sounding sad and faraway.

"Arragh, when I was just a wee boy, I overheard one unlucky Irish farmer describe it to my own Da. I will never forget the way it haunted me each night after that. My imagination went wild and I thought the blight rather resembled a ghost. I heard that old man say, "a queer mist came over the Irish Sea and the potato stalks turned black as soot."[5]

In the year he turned fifteen years old, Da said almost one third of the crop was lost and the small tenant farmers suffered almost immediately. The burgeoning population began to starve and weaken which increased their susceptibility to deadly diseases such as typhus, dysentery and cholera. Recovery from the spreading, malicious diseases depended upon good nutrition, which in Irelands' case, at the time, was inadequate or totally unavailable.

"So you see, sweet baby girl, it wasn't only the musky blight that ruined our soil but the contamination of pestilence it spread and proliferated among us. Circumstances don't arrive just by themselves but come because of consequences. I once complained to my Ma'thair that I had no shoes to wear to church until I met a man on the road who had no feet. I will always remember the lesson I learned that day. Times were tough then, as now, but I count my blessings for the simple things I do have."

Reaching into his back pants pocket, Da carefully extracted and unfolded an old, yellowed newspaper he had saved from his younger days. On the page were the words a fellow by the

---

[5] *Irish Famine Still Haunts Us*, Mulligan, Hugh A., The Evansville Courier, Sunday, Aug. 20, 1995

name of James Mahoney, a Cork County artist, wrote in the London News. Da prayerfully read the story to me, his eyes moist from the memory of the time.

"Listen to this Dehlia. This article is a first- hand account of the devastation."

"I started from Cork, by the mail, for Skibbereen and saw little until we came to Clonakilty, where the coach stopped for breakfast; and here, for the first time, the horrors of the poverty became visible, in the vast number of famished poor, who flocked around the coach to beg alms: amongst them was a woman carrying in her arms the corpse of a fine child, and making the most distressing appeal to the passengers for aid to enable her to purchase a coffin and bury her dear little baby. This horrible spectacle induced me to make some inquiry about her, when I learned from the people of the hotel that each day brings dozens of such applicants into the town.[6]"

Turning his yellowed newspaper around, my Da continued to read. "Listen to this letter to the editor of the Cork Examiner by Jeremiah O'Callaghan."

"Sir: On entering the graveyard this day, my attention was arrested by two paupers who were engaged in digging a pit for the purpose of burying their fellow paupers; they were employed in an old ditch. I asked why they were so circumscribed; the answer was "that green one you see on the other side is the property of Lord Berehaven. His stewards

---

[6] Mahoney, James, Sketches in the West of Ireland, published in the Illustrated London News, 1847

have given us positive directions not to encroach on his property, and we have no alternative but this old ditch; here is where we bury our paupers." I measured the ground—it was exactly 40-feet square and contained, according to their calculation, 900 bodies."

Da stopped a minute to compose himself before he continued reading the article.

"They then invited me to come and see a grave close by. I could scarcely endure the scene. The fragments of a corpse were exposed, in a manner revolting to humanity; the impression of a dog's teeth was visible. The old clothes were all that remained to show where the corpse was laid."[7]

"Arragh child, the harsh days of the Famine were a catastrophe for the poor tenant farmer, unable to feed his family yet bound to the land that had given him birth. Now, I don't want to scare you with talk of death and destruction but ye need to be aware times were hard in the old days."

"Da, I know life was hard for you and your family but my teacher said Ireland was still producing grain crops, enough to feed the population. I don't understand why our people starved and died."

"Oh yes, although the potato crop failed our country was still producing and exporting more than enough grain crops, but that is the crux of the matter! You see, the grain was considered a "money crop" and not a "food crop" and could not be interfered with."

---

[7]Written to the editor by Jeremiah O'Callaghan, from Bantry Abbey, June 12, 1847, and published June 16, 1847) ighm.nfshost.com/letters-to-the-cork-examiner

"But why Da? Why not keep our grain to ourselves?"

"We couldn't darling, a full 75% of our healthy Irish soil was devoted to wheat and oats and other life- saving grains but we had to export it all to England. Those English villains owned the land because the Irish had sold their souls to the devil!"

Seeing the look of shock and dismay on my face, Da stopped his rant.

"I'm so sorry to scare you Dehlia, but you need to know the history of your country. England took over Ireland by a process called, 'submit and regrant.' The evil English would convince, or force, the clan leaders to submit their lands to England and in return were given English titles."[8] "Bah!" Da shook his head as he gazed lovingly at me but with conviction. "Don't let ignorance of the facts define you. Remember this, whatever happens to you in life is a direct result of what you allow to happen, either good or bad."

"But Da, how will I know if something is good or bad for me?"

"Your conscience, Dehlia! Listen to your inner voice, God's voice, to help you along your way. My Mam, God rest her soul, wished for all her children to know the "three sights. May you have hindsight to know where you're been, the foresight to know where you're going and the insight to know when you're going too far! That's my wish for you, too, *Mo Chuisle!*"

Although the famine had ravished Ireland twenty years

---

[8] *The Daughters of Maeve*, Gina Sigillito

"But why Da? Why not keep our grain to ourselves?"

"We couldn't darling, a full 75% of our healthy Irish soil was devoted to wheat and oats and other life- saving grains but we had to export it all to England. Those English villains owned the land because the Irish had sold their souls to the devil!"

Seeing the look of shock and dismay on my face, Da stopped his rant.

"I'm so sorry to scare you Dehlia, but you need to know the history of your country. England took over Ireland by a process called, 'submit and regrant.' The evil English would convince, or force, the clan leaders to submit their lands to England and in return were given English titles."[8] "Bah!" Da shook his head as he gazed lovingly at me but with conviction. "Don't let ignorance of the facts define you. Remember this, whatever happens to you in life is a direct result of what you allow to happen, either good or bad."

"But Da, how will I know if something is good or bad for me?"

"Your conscience, Dehlia! Listen to your inner voice, God's voice, to help you along your way. My Mam, God rest her soul, wished for all her children to know the "three sights. May you have hindsight to know where you're been, the foresight to know where you're going and the insight to know when you're going too far! That's my wish for you, too, *Mo Chuisle*!"

Although the famine had ravished Ireland twenty years

---

[8] *The Daughters of Maeve*, Gina Sigillito

have given us positive directions not to encroach on his property, and we have no alternative but this old ditch; here is where we bury our paupers." I measured the ground—it was exactly 40-feet square and contained, according to their calculation, 900 bodies."

Da stopped a minute to compose himself before he continued reading the article.

"They then invited me to come and see a grave close by. I could scarcely endure the scene. The fragments of a corpse were exposed, in a manner revolting to humanity; the impression of a dog's teeth was visible. The old clothes were all that remained to show where the corpse was laid."[7]

"Arragh child, the harsh days of the Famine were a catastrophe for the poor tenant farmer, unable to feed his family yet bound to the land that had given him birth. Now, I don't want to scare you with talk of death and destruction but ye need to be aware times were hard in the old days."

"Da, I know life was hard for you and your family but my teacher said Ireland was still producing grain crops, enough to feed the population. I don't understand why our people starved and died."

"Oh yes, although the potato crop failed our country was still producing and exporting more than enough grain crops, but that is the crux of the matter! You see, the grain was considered a "money crop" and not a "food crop" and could not be interfered with."

---

[7]Written to the editor by Jeremiah O'Callaghan, from Bantry Abbey, June 12, 1847, and published June 16, 1847) ighm.nfshost.com/letters-to-the-cork-examiner

to send a few coins home every month to provide for all of you here. When you turn eighteen, I will send along enough money for you to join me overseas. Won't you like that Dehlia? Mark my words, we will have such a gay time there!"

The idea of not having Annie to watch over her made Dehlia start to cry harder. She knew she was being selfish but she wanted to stamp her foot down and demand Annie stay home!

"*Ach* now, little Dehlia." Annie soothed. "Remember what the *seanchai*, the storyteller, told us last night about St. Brigid?" Anne asked while wiping Dehlia's eyes and runny nose with a clean but shoddy handkerchief.

Annie tenderly began, "Long, long ago, beautiful Brigid, who remained unwed on purpose, went away with a group of virgins and widows, and together they started a farm and did very well. Of course, Brehon Laws, the ancient laws of Ireland, gave women marital and property rights as well as equal compensation for equal work." Seeing the look of astonishment on Dehlia's face, she continued. "Aye, even daughters had the right to inherit land from their fathers!"

"But those laws don't exist for us today, do they Annie?"

"*Nil*, they do not! Women were emancipated in the 5th and 6th Century. Brigid was born to a pagan King who wed a Christian Slave, and was raised right here in Connacht. Back in those days, the bear, the wolf, and the wildcat roamed all of Ireland. The hungry wolf killed many of the sheep in the meadows. Brigid called the wolf to her, made him stand at her heels, and gave him a big plate of meat and a big bowl of milk. "For that," Brigid stated, "wild animal that you are, you will now guard the flocks from dogs like you and will be with me as my servant and guardian for the rest of my life." And the wolf agreed and he was."[1]

"I know Annie, I know!" Dehlia sobbed louder. "But what does that old story have to do with you leaving us to seek your fortune?"

While settling herself down beside me on our shared bed and enclosing my tiny hands within her calloused ones, Annie patiently explained, "Well now, let me think. Brigid called all the birds of the air and they came to her, and they stayed safe. And when times were hard and she had no flour she called upon her namesake, who was the goddess of fertility and the harvest. The goddess had a vision and ensured her that her crops would be fruitful. All the creatures who were under Brigids' protection flourished. Now the Devil saw all of this happiness and didn't think very much of it so he said, 'I'll put a stop to this!'

But Brigid made a cross out of rushes, and she held it up in front of her and declared, 'Let this cross be the sign of my God so that no devil will come near any house where this cross is held.'

"Dehlia, every year we create our Brigid Cross, made fresh with fragrant rushes. The Cross offers us assurance that each year we may again have fresh protection and a bountiful harvest. So long as you continue to make them, St Brigid will guard Ireland, as well as you! My darling," Annie paused to think of a good analogy. "I guess you could say I am just like

---

[1] *In Search of Ancient Ireland*, McCaffrey, Carmel and Eaton, Leo

before Dehlia was born, she now was able to understand her parents, as well as her grandparents, had suffered incredible losses in those insidious years. Looming all around her were reminders of the Great Famine; graves that had been excavated for fallen family members as well as lonely, deserted homes, workhouse stations and sites of soup-kitchens for the poorest of the poor. Often, while aimlessly wandering across the fields, she discovered traces of undug "lazy beds" in the fields. Invented in her very own province of Connaught, these shallow rows of naked rock and soil enabled the farmers to use a method of arable cultivation where parallel bands of ridges and furrows are dug by spade, resulting in creating narrow and inadequate drainage ditches between them. Cheating only themselves, this method allowed the destitute farmer to glean a cheap and quick harvesting of the potato but unfortunately, allowed the fungus to quickly pass between rows of earth to infiltrate the soil. In Connaught, the small town of Ballyhaunis had been struck the hardest. The black mold blanketed the farmer's fields and smothered the soil. The fungus established a choke-hold on the potato vines, wringing the life out of the farmer's crop as well as his livelihood. Evidence of the murderous blight could still be observed in the empty rows, left fallow by despair.

One night, Dehlia was again listening to her Da describe the hardships his family suffered during the famine years.

"It was so bad, all the people were starving or getting ill from the sickness passing from one forlorn soul to another. The animals didn't have food to eat, but soon we had no livestock, either! We had to sacrifice them to feed our own mouths and then, that was all gone!"

Mam interjected, overhearing Dehlia's Da recount the losses the famine brought with it. "All was not lost, Thomas. Don't forget the parcels of food our Church passed out among us. The good Fathers did not have enough to sustain them as well but they willingly gave to the needy on more than one occasion!"

"Aye, that's true! I remember being the lucky recipient of a few tasty loaves of bread to satisfy my hunger." He acknowledged.

Mam, ever the optimist, warmed to the story, "Ireland's beloved Catholic Church tried to organize equal distribution of food for its' impoverished parishioners but the magnitude of the devastation overwhelmed the priests. Such a pity they weren't able to save all the wee ones!" she sadly added.

Da unfolded yet another yellowed scrap of paper. Dehlia could see that it too, had been opened and closed at least a hundred times before, so wrinkled and torn it was. He read aloud to Dehlia what Father Matthew of Cork, observed and had been quoted in the London News,

"These poor creatures, the country poor, are now homeless and without lodgings; no one will take them in; they sleep out at night. The citizens are determined to get rid of them. They take up stray beggars and vagrants and confine them at night in the market place, and the next morning, send them out in a cart five miles from the town and there they are left and a great part of them perish for they have no home to go to."[9]

Da explained the so-called citizens the good Father was alluding to were the numerous landlords who were split into varying mindsets and degrees of change. Some land owners felt sympathy for the small tenant farmer and tried to ease the burden by looking the other way when the rents were due, but more often than not, the landlords, especially the ones who lived far away in England, made unfair demands on the Irish farmers toiling in the fields for them.

"The wretched "Gregory Clause" of the Poor Law Extension Act of 1847 was toxic and denied aid to anybody owning over a quarter of an acre of land." Da pointed out, "While another equally leveling clause made the landlord responsible for the landholding tax on any holding valued at under four pounds. These two clauses clearly established the numerous smallholders of land as parasites!" he angrily spat out.

"But Da, what were the poor farmers to do?" I asked. "If they didn't have the means to pay taxes on their land because the crops had failed, how were they to survive? It doesn't quite seem fair, does it?"

"No, dear one, it doesn't but there is much in Life that is not fair. As a result, many absent and greedy English landlords used the law to clear their estates of the small Irish farmer or cottier, of which County Mayo was abundantly filled with. Some sympathetic landlords bankrupted

---

[9] Mahoney, James, *Sketches in the West of Ireland*, published in the Illustrated London News, 1847

themselves trying to help their frantic tenants, however, their heroic efforts to stave off disaster for the teetering economy were far and few between." Shaking his head, Da conceded, "I'm afraid "fairness" was not a term frequently used in the old days."

Dehlia eagerly consulted her history books for cross references and parallels to her A'thair's story. She learned the hellish nightmare brought on by the unrest and political implications provoked an exacerbated but failed Irish uprising in 1848, called the Young Irelander Rebellion. Dehlia was surprised to learn, her father had, at one time, been a card-carrying member.

Chapter Three

Agrarian Resurgence

One damp and humid day, too hot for Dehlia to wander through the fields, her mother Margaret asked, "Darling, go into our bedroom and bring your father's worn handkerchiefs back to me to be mended." Wearily sighing to herself and to no one in particular, she whispered, "Work without end is housewife's work."

Racing into her parent's room, glad to be a helper, Dehlia stood on tip-toe and eagerly reached into the top drawer. She yanked out the threadbare cloths from within the usually forbidden contents. When she did, a small rectangle of kelly green tumbled out with them. Picking up the slightly frayed piece of cloth, Dehlia asked, "Mam, what is this tiny ribbon for? Why did you have it tucked among Da's old hankies?"

"Why Child, that small ribbon of fabric is your Da's symbol of defiance, once worn as a badge in his pocket." She gently answered. "Your Da had been a part of a group of brave men who attacked the tithe and process servers who sought to revoke Tenants' Rights. Their group was called The Ribbon Society, hence the smallish token of their resistance worn proudly on the outside of their breast pocket as well as inside their hearts! "

Even though young Dehlia was more interested in romping amongst the hedge-rows and merrily rolling down the soft emerald meadows with her friends, she was aware numerous, insidious, secretive societies proliferated in Ireland just like the wild flowers that grew tucked and protected within the tall grasses of her playground.

The Defenders of the Young Irelander Rebellion had pertinaciously evolved into The Ribbon Society, an agrarian secret society, whose members, like her own father, were rural Irish Catholics. Their living conditions had become miserable after the famine snuck into the fields and smothered the potato crop. The uncaring absentee landlords exercised their terroristic rights, with local farmers and rural workers evicted from their homes by the thousands. The Ribbon Society's objective was to prevent the heartless, money-grubbing landlords from punishing their tenants.

Pausing a minute to choose her words carefully, Margaret continued in a hushed tone, "In the year of 1848, The Young Irelanders launched a rebellion against British rule and the fearless Irish National Land League was formed to defend the interests of the tenant farmers. The Land League demanded from the English government, the Three F's- Fair rent, Free sale and Fixity of tenure for the small tenant farmer who were the vulnerable victims of discrimination."

Dehlia begged her mother to continue. "Please go on Mam, I want to know what Da did! Did he take up the sword and run through the English buggers?"

Sighing just a little, Margaret glanced up at her youngest daughter, wondering where all this gritty information about revolution would settle in Dehlia's mind. She fervently hoped it would not harm her daughter's innocent ways, but by the same token, she knew a child needed to learn the truth about her heritage from her own kin, so she cautiously continued educating Dehlia to the tangled web of rebellion.

"In 1849, when your father was nineteen and on the threshold of becoming an adult, he bravely fought in the Battle of Dolly's Brae! Unfortunately it was a failed battle resulting in Catholic homes burnt and at least 80 Catholics killed." Dehlia's mother gazed off into the distance and quietly stated, not so much as a fact but as a wish, "At least the violence has simmered down for a while now but mark my words, *Mo Chuisle*," she warned, "whenever people are stressed they become more warlike as well as more religious!"

Dehlia instinctively knew that deep down in the warp and welf of her DNA, she too, would fight to avenge injustices and misrepresentations. Hadn't her Da told her nothing is done without effort? And didn't he often tell her she was but a "chip off the ole' block?"

The next year dawned and Dehlia bloomed delicately like a tender young rose on the vine. She grew into a leggy young maid and stopped playing with her dolls. She was twelve years old and "sharp as a tack" as her Da bragged to anyone that would listen! Pretty, as well as intelligent, Dehlia noticed a smidgeon of trouble boiling up among the poor population of Ireland and brewing into a heady revival of social unrest. She heard the murmuring, acrid talk of social injustice. It whirled around her head like an angry tornado and created a dust storm of political dissension. On Sunday, the 20th of

August, 1879, this seething unrest reared its ugly head when land agitation started anew at a town meeting held in County Mayo. While visiting with her friends and walking through town, Dehlia overheard the whisperings of gossips lurking across their fences. She listened and heard them proudly proclaim that fifteen thousand angry Irish had faithfully banded together when they heard of the threat to evict local tenants for arrears of rent from the estate of an absentee English landlord. The buzzing and riotous meeting successfully led, not only to the cancellation of the proposed evictions, but to a general reduction of rents as well for the humble tenants. This lucky meeting of minds was indeed a testament to the Irish Proverb, "two shorten the load."

At last, a little success in the right direction for our poor, hard- working farmers! We have banded together like a close knit family. Dehlia thought to herself with relief. The old timers like my grandparents, used the Triad, a simple memory trick to learn laws and history. Hmm, let's see if I can remember one. She paused for only a second. Ah ha! What are three things that stay longest in a family? Fighting, drinking and red hair! Giggling to herself, Dehlia was proud of the analogy she had made between family and the Irish patriots.

irishhistorypodcast.ie/2011/05/20/an-introduction-to-the-land-war-1879-1882/

In the local Irish papers, Dehlia read brave reports of staunch men like Michael Davitt, James Daly and Charles Parnell, the resilient leaders and defenders of the national Irish movement. She learned these men combined their efforts to reform the Irish land-system and, as a result, the National Land League of Mayo was founded. Unfortunately, their peaceful intentions could not always sway violent aggression, on either side of the situation! Cattle were maimed and property was often destroyed in the turbulent and on-going struggle against the land agents and landlords. Dehlia would often hear the pugilist Irish tenant farmers aggressively proclaim, "A good run is better than a bad stand!"

Dehlias' interest was piqued and she inconspicuously lurked in the shadows of her familys' hearth, hoping to eavesdrop on her parents' musings. This covert activity enabled her to grasp an understanding of current events, which were as slippery as rocks in a gurgling stream. One could locate the stepping stones but it was difficult to anchor a foothold on them, the surfaces scummy and slimy like the righteous indignation of the misunderstood protesters!

One evening she overheard her Da exclaim, "Even though they raped the Irish landscape, at least for once, the English felt our Irish wrath!"

Dehlia gasped, for she knew the evil word "rape" could mean taking someone or something by force, such as the English landlords were doing to the Celtic land. Did the Irish wrath project enough force to stem the tide of the ruthless greed spewed forth by the foreign government? She didn't know but she desperately wanted to find out.

"Da? What are the *"Gombeen"* men?" Dehlia asked the next night before heading off to bed.

"Where did you hear that, Darling?"

"I overheard an irate farmer cussing at the market place. He was angry and pointing out to the clerk that the man walking across the street from them was a *gombeen* man. Then he spit on the street after he said it!"

"Well, that farmer had better watch out! An open mouth often catches a fist! *Gombeen* is the name we have pinned to rural loan sharks. Those awful men slink and lurk amid the countryside and charge fees with exorbitant interest rates. Those so-called, adjusted fees, have brought many a hardworking farmer to their knees when they attempted to pay down their property holdings. Sometimes the poor farmer can't recover and they eventually lose their land to the King's banks."

"I should think the loan sharks would be glad to just get paid in the first place without resorting to charging high interest." Dehlia thought out loud.

"Aye, you would think so, Darling, but remember, the quiet cat also drinks the milk! Sometimes a person will do something they know might not be right, but they do it anyway."

Ever wakeful, Dehlia overheard her parents whispering together late one night, long after they thought everyone was sound asleep.

"Thomas, I don't want you involved with the rebels who crave social change by the use of the sword! I would surely pine away and die if you were carted off to *carcair*."

"Hush now Margaret! I know you don't want me tae land in jail, but how else can we stand up to the English if we don't fight for our rights? It was Thomas Wolfe Tone, the great Irish revolutionary, who proudly said, "Our freedom must be had at all hazards. If men of property will not help us they must fall; we will free ourselves by the aid of that large, respectable class of the community - the men of no property."

Pausing to collect his thoughts, Thomas added, "I see no other way to gain our liberty. Violence, unfortunately, always begets bloodshed."

Print collection of Maggie Land Blanck, London News, January 1, 1881 - The State of Ireland; "Boycotting" A Tradesman, County Mayo January 1, 1881. Clearly boycotting in this instance meant more than not shopping in the store of this tradesman. The townsmen have come out to "groan" and make unpleasant noises and comments.

"Non-violence, Thomas!" Margaret staunchly replied, hands on her hips. "There has been talk in town of a method called ostracisation. Women can lead by not trading with the shop owners who deal with the wretched English landlords and YOU farmers can refuse to bring in the harvest! It might work! We have to try something! I swear, there has been far too much red blood spilt in the name of righteousness! If we don't do something to staunch the flow more martyrs will be created to lead the innocent to their deaths!"

"Anyway Thomas, I worry that all this talk of revolution will negatively influence our children." Margaret declared. "Don't you think I haven't seen our little Dehlia hid in the shadows, listening and observing us and all the other townspeople? She has a nimble mind and wants to know all the ins and outs of this mess! Children learn values at the feet of their parents. We must not be the source of aberrant radicalism!"

"Aye, I hear what ye'r saying Margaret, but Dehlia is a wee girl and having a fine time of 'hide and seek,' that's all!"

"Ach, you're a fine, but dense man Thomas! Don't you know there are three clouds that obscure the sight of wisdom: forgetfulness, ignorance and a little knowledge. Let's just pray Dehlia doesn't use this "new found information" to talk herself into doing something she will later regret!"

"She is a still a wee bairn Margaret, no harm will be done."

And Dehlias' Da was correct, at least for a short period of time. To help keep the angry world at bay and visions of looming violence suppressed, Dehlia would often ask her mother to sing her favorite lullaby to her before drifting off to sleep each night.

"Och Dehlia, you are too old for baby lullabies," her Mother would laughingly croon, "but seein's it soothes you so, I will oblige. After all, *Is buaine port ná glór na n-éan, Is buaine focal ná toice an tsaoil,* a tune is more lasting than the song of the birds, and a word more lasting than the wealth of the world."

"Oh Mam! I love you so much! I don't want to be anywhere in this world except right here with you and Da!"

The melody was so soothing, I often hummed along while listening to my mothers' comforting voice at nightfall.

Lay down your head
And I'll sing you a lullaby
Back to the years
Of loo-li, lai-ley
May there always be angels
To watch over you
To guard you each step of the way
To guard you and keep you
Safe from all harm
Loo-li, loo-li, lai-ley

Indeed, our family might not have had bushels of money, but I felt safe and warm in our small home, in our familiar village, and among our kindred Irish brethren. However, I often paused from my playing to wonder if my parents and the townspeople would ever erase the pinched look of doubt and worry firmly etched upon their faces. If the Heavenly angels in the lullaby were watching over me and keeping me out of harms' way, I was truly grateful for their Grace.

Unfortunately, the land question would not begin to be settled until long after 1880, when I was older and Annie had safely made her way through the Golden Doors of American opportunity.

The years that followed my meandering trek from babyhood to girlhood were often fraught with periods of social unrest between the Irish land workers and the English land owners. When I questioned my Da about this, he would stand still, stroke his scratchy chin and carefully remark, "Aye girl, Ireland has long been a nation used to battling aggression and hostile invasion. Why, from its earliest days Ireland was divided into four tidy quarters, that of Ulster, Leinster, Munster, and Connacht.[10]" It's been recorded in ancient books that the four provinces experienced profound sorrow with blood gushing in their fields when the Vikings first stepped out of their boats and upon Irish soil."

Noticing the alarm registered on my face, Da immediately winked at me and continued, "It has often been said that the Vikings greatest gifts to Ireland were red-heads and cities!" I giggled as he gently patted the top of my sandy-colored head and freckled cheeks.

"Indeed, while both were welcomed," Da paused as he bit his lip, "the Vikings also brought with them the egotistical opinion they were more civilized than the current inhabitants!"

In school, hidden deep within our scholarly yet dilapidated, worn out history books, I learned the Norman Invasion, or as Da would say, the English Invasion, would

---

[10] Wars of the Irish Kings: A Thousand Years of Struggle, from the Age of Myth Through the Reign of Queen Elizabeth, David Willis McCullough

continue to blanket our land of peat and try to snuff out our Celtic autonomy. According to Da, the collapse was an ongoing nightmare looming over all of us.

One day in 5th grade, our astute teacher stiffly remarked, "Normans whose families had settled in Southern Wales after 1066- did indeed sail from there. But whatever its name, the little army that landed on the coast between Waterford and Wexford in 1170, began its first battle against the Irish by driving a herd of captured cattle toward them, and brought English Rule to Ireland."

I perked up my ears! This sounds like fightin' words, for sure! I astutely thought. Letting loose a murderous horde of frightened cattle to stampede over huts and crops would cause a horrific scene of mayhem, indeed!

In my imagination I could hear the Celts loudly shouting as they ran for safe haven, "*Imeacht gan teacht ort*, Go away and don't come back!" but unfortunately for us, the terroristic English were here to stay. Our teacher told us by 1536, Henry VIII had broken with Rome and stubbornly declared himself head of the Church in England and Ireland. Back then, the four unlucky, pugilistic provinces of Ulster, Munster, Leinster and Connaught found themselves wrestling to retain their generational land as well as their Catholic religion.

As I was growing up in the 1870's and 80's, I was acutely aware the island we called Ireland was undergoing immense cultural, social and economic change. In school, we were instructed to learn the English language and resist using Gaelic, the beautiful language of our people. After looking over my school papers, Mam would shake her head side to side and often mutter, "Tsk, tsk! A country without a language is a country without a soul!"

I looked around and noticed some victimized parts of Ireland were still experiencing the rotten, toxic aftereffects of the Great Irish Famine. I also observed most of the people in the four provinces still lived and farmed under the greedy law of the English Lords. I covertly listened to any and all communication, trying to sort out in my innocent head why anyone would be so cruel to their fellow man. Late one night I overhead Da and Mam discussing this fact after the rest of the family had gone to bed.

"Margaret, with the famine less than a generation old, tenant farmers like us will not tolerate the mighty Lords taking our hard earned money and causing our families to starve anymore! We are not prepared to let tragedy strike a second time! Enough is enough!" Da gallantly swore.

"Aye, I hear you Thomas, but God will find a way to deliver us."

"Nay Darling, sometimes I wonder whose side God is really on! I'm afraid that this Landlordism, as they call it, is the teetering downfall of the Irish but the righteous and absolute pillar of British rule! Why, just the other day I picked up this article by the high and mighty Englishman, Charles Kingsley, who has Queen Victoria's ear as her Chaplain. Let me read this smut to you. Scrunching down in the dark corner of the hall and drawing up in a ball so her parents would not detect her presence, Dehlia listened as her Da spoke again.

Clearing his throat of phlegm and straightening out the papers so he could read them in the darkened interior,

Thomas began. "See here, it reads, *'I am daunted by the human chimpanzees I saw along that hundred miles of horrible country.'* "He means us Margaret, don't ye see?" Noticing his wife's shocked face and quiet stillness, Thomas continued reading, *"I don't believe they are our fault. I believe that there are not only many more of them than of old, but that they are happier, better and more comfortably fed and lodged under our rule than they ever were. But to see white chimpanzees is dreadful: if they were black, one would not feel it so much, but their skins, except where tanned by exposure, are as white as ours."*[11]

"Now you see how the World thinks of us? Bah! Kingsley is a *deargnamhaid* and a friend of Charles Darwin! That explains it all! Bah! Everyone is an expert until they speak!"

Stunned, Margaret stopped her darning and set her quaking hands down on her lap in order to absorb the full weight of the words her husband had enlightened her with. After a few minutes of silence, Thomas picked up his thread of discontent once again.

"Our people are determined to organize as a social movement seeking fairer rights on their farms and lands led by an effective tenant leadership. I hear they are going to call themselves The Land League." Wearily shaking his head while lighting his pipe, Da halted a bit, then continued on, "In town there is talk about Michael Davitt, the son of an evicted tenant farmer here in County Mayo, who lost his right arm in a factory accident and is full of righteous indignation! Him

---

[11] Cahill, T., How the Irish Saved Civilization, page 6

and another fellow, by the name of Charles Parnell, are heading this group of activists."

"I think nothing good can come of this, Thomas! Make sure ya do not enter into the fray this time. We have too many mouths to feed now. I don't want to become a lonely widow, lighting a candle every night for your achin' soul to find its' way home! Let Gods' will be done I tell ya!"

I silently crept back to my bed with my Mam's and Da's words echoing in my head. I knew the same thought that challenged my Da's intelligence had also taken root and bloomed in my ma'thirs' consciousness, however, she was more careful to keep her opinion to herself.

The uncensored English news rags were abound with the same brazen attitude toward the rural Irish communities.

Their published words were as sharp as swords and greatly wounded our, already low, self-esteem. As a result, I could see the mired and landless Celtic people often turned to their religion to provide stability and tradition. These were the knots they could cling to as the rope of their daily life became oily and slick with despair.

Then, one hot summer eve, a wondrous event took place in a nearby town that symbolically painted a rainbow of glory onto the canvas of our dreary lives! An Apparition appeared, direct from Heaven's shores, a celestial vision that renewed our common hope in Irish blessings. It was that same slender thread of faith I, myself, clung to when I later became involved in the errant radical adventures of the political melee that directly led to my expulsion from the Isles of green and gold and straight down to the black depths of despair!

Chapter Four

Where Pilgrims Flock

I had heard it asserted, by many adults in town, that Irish lace was world famous for its' intricate designs that develop and form from very simple shapes and patterns. Mam once told me, "Ursuline nuns came from France to devote their lives to work and worship within our churches. They brought with them the skills for weaving Venetian lace. In turn, they diligently taught those of us that had such an aptitude for crocheting. I learned well from these kind sisters when I was but a mere babe as you."

Ignoring my Mam's remark about my youth, I asked her a question that had long been on my mind. "When I visit some of my friends' homes, their nanas and aunties quickly hide their piecework under a cushion. Why are some families so secretive with their patterns? Are they afraid I will copy their designs?"

"Aye, I suppose they do! The jealousy and hoarding of patterns came about right after the famine broke out, when the young, poor Irishwomen only had their skills at the laces to provide some income for their families. The family patterns became guarded secrets from the other lace makers. Hah! Just like you, I have actually seen some lace makers hide their

42 | Journey Through the Half Door

unfinished lace pieces from visitors in an empty chamber pot, sore afraid they were from fear of theft!"

"But *Mai'ther*, most families have a family member each work a portion of the lace, with one skilled in creating flowers, one on leaves and another crocheting the different pieces together using a background mesh. Separate designs that eventually come together to make a beautiful whole, like a loving family, such as ours!"

"Aye darling, they do, indeed! They pass them down from mother to daughter just like curly hair and blue eyes!" Reading the hope in my eyes she added, "And I suppose I could very well teach you all I know too!"

"Oh Mam, you are the best! I can't wait! I promise I will make you proud of me!" I cried, delighted to feel grownup and mature enough to follow our family traditions and ways. Matriculation in school did not give me as much profound pleasure as learning to grasp tendrils of white thread and weave them into objects of such beauty!

Although I was young and my fat, childish fingers clumsy, I learned eagerly and quickly. I was taught crocheted lace "is worked with three different thread weights; a fine thread for the crocheted motifs; a slightly heavier thread is used as a foundation cord; and an even finer thread is used the background netting."[12]

I loved working on the fine netting, looping satiny threads through the open-work to create fine lace collars and cuffs, the designs so indicative of County Mayo. The contemplative

---

[12] *irishcrochetlab.com*

energy it took to skillfully create the lace designs quieted my soul and gave me pause. I often sat peacefully working while recalling some of the letters Annie had faithfully sent to me from America. She had indeed been lucky on the trip across the sea and had obtained a job as a nanny to a wealthy family once she had arrived there. I occasionally re-read the very first letter she wrote to me, so full of hope and triumph.

My Dear, Wee Dehlia,

It was a long and arduous journey across the Atlantic but I arrived at Castle Garden in Manhattan, New York, a little thinner and weaker that when I last left your sight, but buoyed at my prospects in this new world of abundance. As we were crossing the sea, I began a conversation onboard with a dentist who had sadly lost his wife to illness while visiting Europe. As luck would have it, he seemed to approve of my literacy and composure so upon embarking on solid ground, the good doctor sought me out and I was immediately engaged as a nanny for his darling little boy, Henry. I could not believe my good fortune! We will stay for a short time in New York City until Doctor Flickinger has his home in St. Louis, Missouri prepared for our arrival.

I miss you Mo chroi, My heart! I wish I could tuck you inside of my apron pocket so you could peek out at all the comings and goings in this big city! In February a wonderful emporium was opened here, called the "five and dime" store, by a man named Frank Woolworth. All the items are priced at five cents! Can you imagine that? One may simply enter the premises and purchase what one wishes, quite reasonably,

with no haggling or arguing allowed! In time I may have
enough money saved to treat myself to a small goodie or two.
In the meantime, I am sending some of my salary to help
Mam and Da buy you a new pair of shoes. I know you must
be growing by leaps and bounds! Slan go foill! Bye for now!
    Annie

I remember remaining excited and grateful for weeks after
receiving Annie's letter as well as the gold coins enclosed
inside to purchase my new shoes but soon the long and
tiresome hours began to creep back in and consume my life
once again. The days stretched out into a numbing pattern of
doing morning chores, walking to school, studying for four
hours learning English and then shuffling back home to
chores again.

Then, one evening in August, our mundane core of human
existence changed forevermore. The local newspapers
reported a magnificent event in the town of Knock, just seven
miles north of our home. Under the south gable of the Knock
Parish Church, fifteen witnesses, all between the ages of five
and seventy-five years of age, perceived an Apparition of the
Blessed Mary! She was beautifully dressed in glowing white,
while St. Joseph and St. John stood on each side of her.

I thought, Could it be so? Had the Blessed Virgin come to
right the wrongs done to our people? Were our hardships and
tears be vindicated at last?

The papers reported that the witnesses watched the
Apparition in steadily pouring down rain for two hours while
reciting the Rosary. They mentioned that although they were

drenched not a single drop of rain fell on the colorful vision! The next day the local authorities isolated all of the witnesses from each other and instructed them to each testify on what they saw. I particularly liked the account given in the newspapers by plucky Mary Byrne, at the First Commission of enquiry of 1879. I read it over and over, eagerly, looking for Divine instruction.

"I live in the village of Knock, to the east side of the chapel. Mary McLoughlin came on the evening of the 21st of August to my house at about half past seven o'clock. She remained some little time.

I came back with her as she was returning homewards. It was either eight o'clock or a quarter to eight at the time. It was still bright. I had not heard from Miss McLoughlin about the vision, which she had seen just before that.

The first I learned of it was on coming at the time just named from my mother's house in company with Miss Mary McLoughlin, and at the distance of three hundred yards or so from the church, I beheld, all at once, standing out from the gable, and rather to the west of it, three figures which, on more attentive inspection, appeared to be that of the Blessed Virgin, St. Joseph and St. John. That of the blessed Virgin was life-size, the others apparently either not so big or not so high as her figure.

They stood a little distance out from the gable wall and, as well as I could judge, a foot and a half or two feet from the ground.

The Virgin stood erect, with eyes raised to Heaven; her hands elevated to the shoulders or a little higher, the palms inclined slightly towards the shoulders or bosom. She wore a large cloak of a white color, hanging in full folds and somewhat loosely around her shoulders, and fastened to the neck. She wore a crown on the head, rather a large crown, and it appeared to me somewhat yellower that the dress or robes worn by Our Blessed Lady.

In the figure of St. Joseph the head was slightly bent, and inclined towards the Blessed Virgin, as if paying her respect. It represented the saint as somewhat aged, with grey whiskers and grayish hair.

The third figure appeared to be that of St. John the Evangelist. I do not know, only I thought so, except the fact that at one time I saw a statue at the chapel of Lecanvey, near Westport, County Mayo, very much resembling the figure, which stood now before me in group with St. Joseph and Our blessed Lady, which I beheld on this occasion.

He held the book of Gospels, or the Mass Book, open in his left hand, while he stood slightly turned on the left side towards the altar that was over a little from him, I must remark that the statue which I had formerly seen at Lecanvey chapel had no mitre on its head, while the figure which I now beheld had one, not a high mitre, but a short set kind of one. The statue at Lecanvey had a book in his left hand, and the fingers of the right hand raised. The figure before me on this present occasion of which I am speaking had a book in the left hand, as I stated, and the index finger and the middle finger of the right hand raised, as if he were speaking, and impressing some point forcibly on an audience. It was this coincidence of figure and pose that made me surmise, for it is only an opinion, that the third figure was that of St. John, the beloved disciple of Our Lord, but I am not in any way sure what saint or character the figure represented, I said, as I now expressed, that it was St. John the Evangelist and then all the others present said what I stated.

The altar was under the window, which is in the gable and a little to the west near the centre, or a little beyond it. Towards this altar St. John, as I shall call the figure, was looking, while he stood at the Gospel side of the said altar, which his right arm inclined at an angle outwardly, towards the Blessed Virgin. The altar appeared to be like the altars in use in the Catholic Church, large and full-sized. It had no linens, no candles, nor any special ornamentations; it was only a plain altar.

Above the altar and resting on it was a lamb and around it I saw golden stars, or small brilliant lights, glittering like jets or glass balls, reflecting the light of some luminous body. I remained from a quarter past eight to half past nine o'clock. At the time it was raining. Mary Byrne, age 29, testimony of Apparition"[13]

After reading and gleaning all the excitement from the newspaper accounts of the miraculous Apparition citing, my friends and I gathered together after school, eager to gossip and discuss the spectacular event.

"It's indeed a wonderful blessing on our people!" said my good friend Mauve.

"Yes!" exclaimed Colleen, another girlhood friend who

---

[13] *knock-shrine.ie/history*

romantically believed in legends. "Mary herself came to remind us that she is a heavenly messenger from her son, Jesus the Christ, who is divine and can cure us of all our sicknesses and ills. Surely she was sent to help us?"

"Oh to be sure! The visions were sent to us to let us know our lives matter to Him." I stated emphatically. Remember our Religion teacher told us about the Book of Kells, the illuminated text of the Gospels, created by the monks in 800 A.D. They had the unique vision to inscribe the New Testament in that manuscript. It is truly a work of art and a beautiful symbol of our national culture and pride. That is the power of learning!" I exclaimed with fervor. "I think the Apparition that Mary Byrne glimpsed has come to resurrect the belief that flesh does not decay!"

"Aye Dehlia, I agree with you!" Colleen declared. "Isn't the Book of Kells the complete text of the Gospels of Matthew, Mark, Luke and John?"

"Of course it is!" Maeve added. "And the vision of St. John at the altar has come to remind us our struggles will be soon over!"

In my heart, I earnestly wanted to believe my friends and I were right. Ireland needed a small miracle and the vision brought stability and tradition to a society utterly bewildered by change.

Christ holding a Gospel Book (folio 32v)
Photograph: The Board of Trinity College,
Dublin

"Ach," retorted Michael Fagan, fearlessly sidling up to the group, "you are all such silly girls! Don't ya know the Apparition is merely a frivolous idea to confuse us and cloud our minds? It's meant to take our thoughts away from fighting for our rights! By glory, we should continue to strive forward and capture our land back from the English bastards! Why, St. John was glimpsed at Mary's side and don' ye know what happened to him? He was beheaded by a traitor!" Looking at our shocked faces, Michael continued with his appraisal. "Anyway, everyone knows that the Book of Kells was produced purely for artistic appearances rather than practicality."

"Yes, I suppose you're right Michael, but even you have to admit Ireland has been able to produce some of the most beautiful and magical books the world as ever seen." I stated in my typical, stubborn manner.

I carefully observed Michael, so fetching and radiant with his smoldering eyes flashing fire! I experienced a secret, tantalizing desire to follow him to the very ends of the Earth! Puppy love had jumped up and bitten my heart with a vengeance. Even though Michael was a bit older, we had attended school together for many years. I thrillingly began to visualize him as the handsome and dashing man he would eventually mature into and I was amazed to find he showed a little interest in me as well!

There is a wise saying that love is blind and over the next few years I vowed to unequivocally believe what Michael accepted to be true, following the leader, like the lemmings that carelessly plunge over the cliffs to their deaths. I became, a sort of "Molly Maguire", a feminine anchor in a politically active society, one that was hell bent on establishing Home Rule by pugnacious indignation. How often I was reminded of His Word in Psalm 30: verse 5;

"His anger lasts only a moment, but His kindness lasts for a lifetime. Crying may last for a night, but joy comes in the morning."

Surely our righteous anger mired within the revolutionary movement would serve a purpose now so that, in the future, Michael and I could marry and be allowed the opportunity to peacefully raise our own wee brood of children. I only realized much later this antagonistic belief was as fragile as the netting I created lace on. By then it was too late! We might have been better served if we would have heeded the common Irish phase; *"Lie down with dogs and you'll rise with fleas."*

Chapter Five

Mago, God Help Us

In 1882, I received yet another letter from my sister Annie in America. She described her new homeland as a promising, hopeful place, far removed from the County Mayo I knew and lived in, a heady, bubbling brew of turmoil and strife. As I read her stories of what she was experiencing in America, I found myself wondering if she remembered our commonwealths' struggle for liberation. Did she even care about the mired devastation of the luckless Irish countrymen? Annie wrote glibly and seemed to have forgotten the hardships of her Celtic people. She wrote:

My deirflur dhil, or as they say here in America, cherished sister.

My head is all a-whirl with the giddy promises America holds for me and my little charge, Henry Flickinger. Henry, I should remind you, is the Doctor's motherless son, who is now my obligation to help raise and educate. It befalls on me to attend to his every need, or at least those that a small lad of four craves! I have fortunately been able to loan him my stout lap to rest upon and a steady hand to hold. He is a most resilient young boy. We made it safely to St. Louis, a growing city of immigrants of all kinds, German, Polish,

Italian and of course, Irish. I am happily living in a grand house, close to the Mississippi River. Oh my child, it has been astonishing to watch all the growth and productivity this town is experiencing! Why, can you imagine watching an elephant being led across a wide bridge to test its' strength? With my very own eyes, I saw a large gray elephant cross the newly completed Eads Bridge. It is commonly believed that elephants have instincts that keep them from setting a single foot on an unsafe structure. When that huge mammal boldly traipsed over the steel arches of the bridge, a big crowd cheered and followed him triumphantly over to the Illinois side of the river! What a gay parade followed the event! I have sent you this postcard of the giant bridge, drawn by an artist, right before the parade. It is truly a marvel to behold!

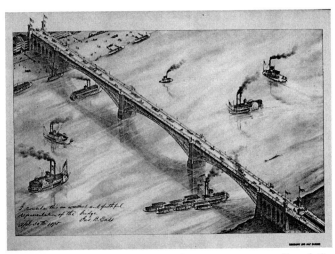

Image of Pictorial St. Louis, the great metropolis of the Mississippi valley; a topographical survey drawn in perspective A.D. 1875 (public domain)

I hope you are minding Mam and Da and not giving your brothers and sister a hard time of it. Remember to carefully mind your stitches in your needlework and don't get distracted by the politics of the day. Be of good cheer! I have discovered that Irish lace is considered a much coveted article of fashion and much sought after among the rich ladies in America. They lovingly adorn their collars and cuffs with the silky cut-work. Perhaps your fortune will be made pursuing this endeavor when I am financially able to send for you. Let me remind you, de reir a cheile a thogtar na caisleain, "it takes time to build castles", but rest assured darling, I am putting money aside and each month the pile grows larger! Please practice your crocheting each night after chores. I am sure by now you have heavenly skills to prove just how fearless you are when you attempt any endeavor! Give Mam and Da a sweet "pog" from their eldest daughter! Let them know that Irish angels are indeed watching over me, keeping me safe and sound.

Much love until we meet again!
Annie

Even though I looked forward to receiving letters from Annie, I eventually grew weary reading of my sister's glorious experiences and her futile hopes for my future. In contrast to Annie living so carefree and liberated over in America, back here at home, Michael had grown darker, more defiant and militant with each passing year. As a result of his influence, I also became ensnared by his rebellious fervor and attempted to mirror his enthusiasm for immediate change in the status quo. At his suggestion, I eagerly joined the Ladies

Land League, the first organized, as well as recognized, engagement of women in politics. Mam's dire predictions of bloody uprisings were now coming true! When many of the male Land League organizers were imprisoned, the Ladies stepped in to help resist evictions and increase solidarity. We banded together to inspire our countrymen to act, however, we did not wish for mayhem to ensue.

When our League founder, Fanny Parnell wrote her poem, *"Hold the Harvest"*, and successfully published it, I, as well as the typical Irish peasant rose up and became enraged, as well as empowered, by her words. Although Fanny had cut her teeth at an early age on her American mothers' roots of anti-slavery and women's rights, she failed to realize her writings would also continue stirring up the angst of young men like Michael, who needed only a worthy cause in order to brandish their weapons in the air and soar anew to challenge injustice!

Hold the harvest

Now are you men, or are you kine, ye tillers of the soil?
Would you be free, or evermore the rich man's cattle toil?
The shadow of the dial hangs that points the fatal hour—
Now hold your own! Or, branded slaves, forever cringe and cower.

The serpent's curse upon you lies—ye writhe within the dust,
Ye fill your mouths with beggers' swill, ye grovel for a crust!
Your lords have set their blood-stained heels upon your shameful heads,
Yet they are kind—they leave you still their ditches for your beds!

Oh! by the God who made us all—the seigneur and the serf—
Rise up! and swear, to hold this day your own green Irish turf;
Rise up! and plant your feet as men where now you crawl as slaves,
And make your harvest fields your camps, or make of them your graves.

Mother Ireland

Vain, ah vain is a woman's prayer!
Vain is a woman's hot despair!
Naught can she do, naught can she dare—
I am a woman, I can do naught for thee, Ireland, mother!

Hold the Harvest and *Mother Ireland* written by Fanny Parnell

The Ladies Land League met frequently amid hostility from all sides. Government forces, the Catholic Church, and the Irish Press, all worked separately to hinder the brisk role the League was claiming in the lives of the people. Fanny "trained rural women to come out of their homes and play an active role in withholding rent, boycotting, and resisting eviction. When resistance failed, she organized the provision of temporary housing and support for those evicted."

The Royal Irish Constabulary dispersing a meeting of the Ladies' Land League. (Illustrated London News, 24 December 1881)

I must admit, I willingly volunteered and did my fair share to move the cause for Home Rule forward. Fanny believed physical war-mongering was not an acceptable solution to the Land problem, however, her violently worded sentences urged many men and women to rally against British rule and subordination. The words of the poverty-stricken Celtic population became sharp and laden with poisoned thoughts. Tempers were frayed and easily caught fire. My

Mam and I agreed with Miss Parnell's patriotic truths but my *mai'ther* did not hold with the manipulation of people's emotions for the exploding cause of Irish freedom. Ever the peace-keeper, Mam held to the supposition of peaceful cooperation among the policy makers and among the courts of law. I often argued that point with her.

"I don't think keeping quiet is going to change the way we are governed, Mam!" stomping my foot down in the dirt for emphasis.

"Perhaps not, Dehlia, but we must uphold the policy makers and hope they can bring fair and balanced change to our land."

"That will take too long! You know that as well as I do!"

"Yes, Dear One, change does take time but going through proper channels is the only way to do it. Anything else brings anarchy and sheds innocent blood."

Unfortunately for all of us, blood-shed did indeed increase in the beleaguered rural areas of Ireland. The sharp sword of discontent was brandished by protesting young gallants who swore to right the wrongs incited by the British government and absentee landowners. The blade of that double-edged saber swiftly sliced my world in two when Michael, now eighteen years old, took the oath of the Irish Republican Brotherhood. He proudly repeated it to me one afternoon when we had a chance to sneak away from our chores and meet in secret at a *Fulacht fiadh,* a mound of burned stone and rock.

It has been "said that one cannot walk a hundred yards through Ireland's countryside without tripping over some kind of ancient monument, but no monuments are more common than the *fulacht fiadh.*"[14] These ancient open-air cooking pits were our favorite natural picnic benches among the heath. Michael and I would sit closely beside each other on loaf-shaped stones, our feet firmly planted in the driest well with thoughts of our lips touching with delight. We were young and innocent, merely children gloriously entwined, hearts as well as hands, covertly plotting our lofty future together. I was pleased to think the ethereal fairies the old people said inhabited the stone circles were applauding our clandestine meetings. After all, even the most superstitious would admit the fairies only appeared to the pure of heart! Of course, I for one embodied nothing but a pure love for Michael and he, well, in my mind's eye, could do no wrong!

Michael leaned over and we sat for some time, shoulder to shoulder, hearts pounding a glorious, steady rhythm within our chests from the closeness of our youthful bodies.

"Dehlia", he whispered, as he squeezed my hand so hard I winced, "listen to this! I'm so proud to say I can now serve others and uphold our cause by doing my part in the services of the Irish Republican Brotherhood! I have memorized the oath and committed it to memory in only one night! I plan on taking the pledge tomorrow at our regular meeting with some of the other men who have volunteered. Would you like to hear it?" he asked with a sparkle in his eye.

"Aye, I would Michael." I answered a little reluctantly, for I knew the Devil was in the details.

---

[14] *In Search of Ancient Ireland,* page 43

Michael pulled himself up as straight and unyielding as the hard stones that lay scattered all around us. He proudly began:

I, Michael Fagan, in the presence of Almighty God, do solemnly swear allegiance to the Irish Republic, now virtually established; and that I will do my very utmost, at every risk, while life lasts, to defend its independence and integrity; and, finally, that I will yield implicit obedience in all things, not contrary to the laws of God, to the commands of my superior officers. So help me God. Amen."[15]

Isn't that a wonderful and stirring promise?" Michael asked, as he happily plopped back down onto our sturdy rock ledge. "We call ourselves a military organization. What I just told you was the legionary oath all of us soldiers promised to the cause!" he reverently added while smiling blissfully.

"Aye, you are so brave!" I said with conviction, for I would have followed him into oblivion, I was so smitten. "But Michael," I said as I stamped my foot down in the bitter dirt, dust whirling around my calf. "Do you realize you are pledging your life to a secret organization that upholds justice by any means? Why, you could lose your life!" I managed to stammer out, suddenly realizing the seriousness of the situation. The tentacles of that terror invaded my mind as sure as the roots of a mighty oak tree grow downward into the soil! I had not imagined the provocative thought of rebellion to expose Michael to an untimely death!

Michael just continued to stare through me with a faraway

---

[15] oath written by Thomas Clarke Luby, *wikipedia.org/wiki/Irish_Republican_Brotherhood.*

look of naked, utter conviction. I quickly discerned he would not be satisfied until he had served his nation in some way, so I tried another tactic to convince him to abandon these principles of brash anarchy. Bribery had always worked well in our household, so I attempted that.

"Anyway, I won't continue to meet with you in secret as you do with your fellow soldiers!" I haughtily tossed out there. "I want to be able to walk out with you and let my brother Austin chaperone as "daisy picker"! Don't you want to woo me and make me your wife, forever and ever?" I asked, but when I noticed Michael was not taking the bait, I jumped straight up and cried out, unashamed, "Michael, I want to have a public courtship and be done with these secretive meetings!" Tangy tears of desperation began to roll down my cheeks. Alarmed that he had hurt my feelings with his heroic obsession, Michael sprung up as well and tenderly grabbed ahold of my arms.

"Oh aye Dehlia, I do too!" he pledged, his eyes all velvety and soft. "I do want to court you the proper way and marry you on the favored day as well. Let's see," he said with a twinkling gleam in his eye, "how does that silly rhyme go? Monday for health, Tuesday for wealth, Wednesday the best day of all. Thursday for losses, Friday for crosses, and Saturday, no day at all!" We both doubled over in childish laughter and then Michael surprised me by trying to steal a gentle *pog* from me. But I was much too nimble for his kisses and romantic advances!

"Why Michael Fagan," I reproached him, glancing up sideways with my eyes flirtatiously. "Don't you know you have to "walk the land" and let my parents inspect your family home before I allow you to kiss me?"

Michaels' face immediately darkened and took on a seriousness as he looked down to the ground. *"Ta bro norm,* Dehlia, I'm sorry. I don't have any land for your parents to survey. All the parcels of our family property have already been divided up between my older brothers. Da has stated my younger sister and I are obliged to remain unmarried and continue to work our land for the good of the family." He raised his gaze just in time to see large tears begin to bloom in my eyes.

"Do you mean we can never get married Michael?" I asked. "Why have we been making plans to wed then? Has your passion all been a sham?"

"Nil Dehlia. My feelings for you have been true, as yours have been for me but reality is hard to ignore. I am the least favored son of a poor family and merely a pauper, with no hopes of owning land. I don't know how to support myself, much less a pretty little lass like you as a wife!"

"Oh Michael, I feel so foolish! I've loaned you my heart and all you have given back to me are empty promises of favored days and foolishness!"

"Don't fear Dehlia." Michael gently implored. "By golly, I'll make a vow to you right now! I'm goin' to seek my fortune by fighting to reclaim our rights to Irish soil! I will do my utmost to win our land back from the absentee English landlords and those dirty process servers! Mark my words! May the Devil make a ladder of my back bones while picking apples in the garden of hell! I shall wrestle some acreage from the unjust landlords, some good workable Irish land, then we can set up our own housekeeping!"

He looked at me and saw my doubt, as well as my fear for the potent force of his strong words and conviction. After all, every dog is brave on his own doorstep. Recovering my composure, I struggled to paint a smile on my face and mirror his conviction.

"Oh my beauty!" Michael implored. "Can you not wait for the good times to unfold? Surely you know these things do take time? Are you willing to take a chance on me?"

"Oh aye Michael, I do believe you'll find a way for us to be together. I just wish there was more I could do for the cause of Irish freedom than sit at home and twiddle my thumbs! Boycotting tradesmen and delivering secrets seems such a tame way of fighting for independence from tyranny."

"Bonny Dehlia, you are just as important to the cause as anyone. Each of us have our parts to play in the grand scheme of things. I would not like to see that pretty little head of yours swinging from a gallows." Gallantly he cried, "Leave it to us men to raise our swords and cut the knees out from under the enemy!"

If only I could have peered into a crystal ball to predict and take action to halt the calamity of the future rolling and tumbling towards us. If only the angels in my mother's lullaby could have curbed the wheels that were grinding down the path towards our final destination.

I knew Michael, the handsome and sunny boy, as well as the dark and stormy man he had become. And I knew he was a loose cog in the gearwheel of his family hierarchy. He was often reckless and rash. That kind of errant behavior soon drove him to become involved with a more radical breakaway faction. They called themselves the Irish National Invincibles.

The Irish Land League Agitation: Attack on a Process Server. The Illustrated London News, July 30, 1881, (The artist was Aloysius O'Kelly born Dublin, Ireland, 1851 died 1936)

The seed of the sticky feeling of doom I experienced grew ever so deep inside the pit of my stomach. I had much to be afraid of for I soon read in the local newspaper the British government had taken action against the rebels by introducing the Coercion Act. It was meant to pacify the conservative people of Ireland and yet discourage dissension from Irish nationalists such as Michael Davitt and Charles Stuart Parnell, who were central figures in the movement. The Act was harsh for it suspended Habeas Corpus, or trial by jury and proclaimed entire districts as radical and "disturbed", thereby opening the political gate to allow the governing "powers that be" to arrest most of the members of the Land League. The disastrous Act was endorsed by the British governments' most important administrator in Ireland, the Chief Secretary in Dublin Castle by the name of William Forster, "nicknamed "Buckshot" by the Nationalist press, on the supposition that he had ordered its use by the police when firing on a crowd."[16]

We didn't know it then but Fate would arrange for Michael and I to meet for one of the very last times. We eagerly greeted each other one musty evening at our favorite pit in the countryside. I noticed his eyes were burning red and his first words abrasive. They were not the soft tones of adoration I desperately I wanted to hear that night.

"Dehlia," Michael shouted out when he glimpsed me walking toward him over the hillside. I gingerly stepped around the piled stones of the cairn that lay between us. He waved his arms vigorously. "Listen to this! Some nine hundred members of our Land League have been unfairly interned in prison! Mr. Parnell has been thrown in jail as well. It's a travesty of justice! We have to do something!"

---

[16] *en.wikipedia.org*

"I know Michael, but what can you do to save them?"

"Why, we will fight, fair colleen, to the death if we have to! I have joined a new fighting group, called the Invincibles. I mean to work underground if need be! You would not believe the senseless slaughter I witnessed in the town of Ballina!" Michael screeched. "I was at the rally and before I knew it, guns were shooting into the crowd, injuring and killing innocent people to the right and left of me! I don't know how they missed me but by God, the Virgin Mary must have been looking over me, saving me for a better purpose!"

"Oh Michael, please don't try to right all the wrongs from the past thirty years all by yourself!" Dehlia pleaded with tears beginning to well up in her eyes.

"Nay, I won't. I have a solid group of like- minded fellows to keep my back! After all, a friend's eye is a good mirror and we all think alike, my pretty."

Michael and I absent-mindedly hugged each other because his thoughts were claimed elsewhere and I was praying to God he would not act upon his righteous anger. After smothering my fear in front of Michael and tacking on a brave face, I ran back home and questioned my *Da*, the authority, on all things I didn't understand, about the Ballina murders.

"Aye darling," my Da began, scratching his head as he wondered how to explain the bloody mess to me. "You know the British Prime Minister?" he asked.

"Yes, yes, William Gladstone is it?" I replied.

"Aye, talk of the Devil, and he will appear! Mr. Gladstone established a land court but unfortunately did not make it applicable to tenant farmers who were in arrears or in debt.

Of course, ye know most of our populace are in that suspended state?"

"Aye, I know all too well. Go on Da!"

"Well, our man Parnell was eventually released from his imprisonment under the terms of the so-called "Kilmainham Treaty", agreeing to use his influence to calm the violent land agitation that followed the fraudulent court decision. Indignant and outraged by Parnell's release, old Buckshot resigned in protest and was soon replaced by one Frederick Cavendish, the husband of Gladstone's niece."

"What did that mean? That should have been a good thing for evil Mr. Forester to be replaced, right?"

"Not necessarily Dehlia, one wrong does not deserve another. Anyway, an honest authority figure does not place a relative in a position of power. I believe the word for that is "nepotism.""

"I don't understand, Da, Catholic popes in Italy have distributed assignments to their relatives for years. Everyone knows that! How does that make ne-nepotism wrong?"

"Arragh child, easily explained. The pope's canna marry and beget children so their nephews are granted Cardinal positions to move the Pope's political climate in the right direction. I don't think the Church is wrong going in that direction, but the English are another matter!"

"What happened next Da, did this Mr. Cavendish straighten things out?"

"Nil, the old boiling pot of distrust and impatience was stirred the day before Cavendish even arrived on the shores of Ireland! The mood of the time was tense and the Royal Irish

Constabulary, who took their orders from the British, and "Buckshot" Forester, unwittingly fired on a crowd of rowdy but unarmed group of protesters in the town of Ballina. Unfortunately killing several innocent children under the age of fourteen. Tis' such a pity when adult insolence becomes the norm and faultless youngsters are struck down before their prime!"

Dehlia felt her hands get clammy and her heart flutter wildly. So it was true! She had a sickening feeling Michael might try to avenge the senseless murders for he believed it was better to try than to hope.

True enough, late that night, Michael threw up tiny pebbles against her family's kitchen window, startling her as she was cleaning up for her tired Mam.

"Why Michael! What are you doing here so late? Can't stay away from me and my beautiful smile?" Dehia joked half-heartedly, almost afraid to ask.

"No, dear heart, I have but a favor to ask of you. Do you have a sharp knife or tool to loan your bonny boy for a day or two?" He whispered under the cloak of darkness.

At first, I couldn't comprehend why he would need a blade so badly but I think deep in my unconsciousness I knew it would lead to nothing good. I withheld my reservations for I did not want to disappoint Michael. Why, he meant the World to me! When he asked me to secretly slip a sharp knife out of our kitchen and into his eagerly waiting hands, I did as he asked. Little did I realize then, I had apprehensively committed myself to the bloody reprisal that was about to take place. Looking back, I see that my decision to procure the weapon was the first tangled black knot of thread on the back of my life's' quilt. I would trip on many more knots of pain before my tapestry was completed!

The next day was the sixth of May, 1882. Cavendish and his new chief secretary, Thomas Henry Burke, had arrived in Dublin and were leisurely strolling through Phoenix Park on their way to the Viceregal Lodge, the residence of the Lord Lieutenant of Ireland, Lord Spencer. Just inside the park's entrance, the two Englishmen were approached by a cluster of seven men, three in front, two in the middle and two behind. The first three men turned around and began to stab Cavendish and Burke, brutally assassinating them on the spot. All seven men successfully escaped but the militant group soon contacted all the major newspapers proudly identifying themselves as the Invincibles, the so called "terrorists." Preposterously, the Invincibles had attacked and killed the wrong man! It was Buckshot Foresters' life they had wished to cut down, not the newly appointed Cavendish! The brutality and the swiftness of the murder shocked many people on both sides of the political aisle. I gradually discovered that my reckless Michael was one of the seven murderers and the knife that I thought I had so cleverly stolen from our home was found by the authorities and identified as one fashioned and often used in County Mayo. I had unwittingly involved myself, my family, and our fellow neighbors as well. For a short time I made myself a further accomplish by hiding Michael in the bog below our fields and supplied him with food while mass "Fenian" activists, as they were called by the British political establishment, were arrested and thrown in jail to rot. My Michael was safely hidden but he was adamant about formulating a plan to free his comrades in crime. I thought it was pure foolishness but Michael was ruthless and determined to carry on the campaign against the English authorities. One morning, I found his hiding place empty, the warm blankets I had provided for his bed, cold to the touch. He was gone and my heart began to break into jagged little pieces like a vase when it falls off a high ledge, only to splinter on impact with the hard floor.

A few months later more murders took place in Galway when the same secret society of Invincible's brutally murdered an entire family in an incident linked to land tensions. Da was so right when he said "two wrongs don't make a right!" Meanwhile, in the countryside, many more unsympathetic British landowners were also stalked and murdered, often set upon and killed before they could reach the safety of their homes. These events served to create a climate where political violence was now less tolerable to people on **both** sides of the issue. The chilly months of winter passed us by with no word of Michaels' whereabouts. In March, 1883, I gleaned from the neighborhood gossips that a Special Forces Unit, called the London Metropolitan Police Special Irish Branch, was formed to investigate the Irish Republican Brotherhood, of which the Invincible's were a small fraction of. Where was Michael? Was he out of harm's way or most likely, in the thick of it?

Each evening I furtively read the papers for the latest news. I learned the hunt for the perpetrators of The Phoenix

Park murders was shrewdly led by Superintendent John Mallon, a Catholic from Armagh, who used his suspicions and connections to pit one suspect against another. He was shrewd and brilliantly collected all the names of the Invincibles who had been involved in the crimes. One by one the men were rounded up, James Carey, Michael Kavanagh, Joe Hanlon, Joe Brady, Thomas Caffrey, Dan Curley, Tim Kelly and of course, young, handsome Michael Fagan. Within a few short months they were all brought to trial, convicted of murder and hanged in Dublin.

The last to swing from the gallows was my Michael.

Just before the noose was strung around his neck, Michael's cohort in crime, brave Dan Curley, made a rousing speech to stand infamously in Irish history. It was published in the local newspaper, where I read it, and distributed among the populace. I knew in my heart that Michael would have found agreement in his words. Curley said:

"You will have to be very cautious my lord, about the informers. I don't seek redress. Of course I expect no mercy. I don't pray for pardon. I expect none from the British government; they are my avowed enemies... I know the position in which I am standing here. I am standing on the brink of the grave. I will speak the truth... I admit I was sworn into the Fenian organization twelve years ago; when I was only twenty-two years of age, and from that time to the present I worked openly in the organization. I was let into a number of their secrets, and I will say here today that I will bring them to my grave faithfully and truly; and as to my own life, if I had a thousand lives to lose, I would rather lose them sooner then bring to my grave the name of informer and that I should save my life by betraying my fellow man... I am a member of the Invincible Society – undoubtedly, unhesitatingly."[17]

A new tune, based on a poem written by Charles Joseph Kickham, a Fenian journalist and poet, in tribute to the men who had been betrayed, was soon heard sung in pubs and Catholic homes alike. It was called "Rory of the Hills" and it went something like this[18]:

> "THAT rake up near the rafters, Why leave it there so long?
> The handle, of the best ash,
> Is smooth and straight and strong; And, mother, will you tell me,
> Why did my father frown, When to make the hay, in summer-time
> I climbed to take it down? "She looked into her husband's eyes,
> While her own with light did fill, "You'll shortly know the reason, boy!" Said Rory of the Hill.
>
> Next day the ashen handle
> He took down from where it hung, The toothed rake, full scornfully,
> Into the fire he flung; And in its stead a shining blade
> Is gleaming once again — (Oh! for a hundred thousand of
> Such weapons and such men!) Right soldierly he wielded it,
> And—going through his drill— " Attention "—" charge "—"
> front, point"— "advance"
> Cried Rory of the Hill.
>
> She looked at him with woman's pride,

---

[17] theirhistory.com/2012/07/31/the-invicibles-and-the-phoenix-park-killings
[18] traditionalmusic.co.uk/gt-irish-songs-lyrics1/gt-irish-songs-lyrics10576.htm

With pride and woman's fears; She flew to him, she clung to him,
And dried away her tears; He feels her pulse beat truly,
While her arms around him twine— "Now God be praised for your stout heart,
Brave little wife of mine." He swung his first-born in the air,
While joy his heart did fill — "You'll be a FREEMAN yet, my boy,"
Said Rory of the Hill.

Oh! knowledge is a wondrous power,
And stronger than the wind; And thrones shall fall, and despots bow,
Before the might of mind; The poet and the orator
The heart of man can sway, And would to the kind heavens
That Wolfe Tone were here to-day! Yet trust me, friends, dear Ireland's strength —
Her truest strength—is still, The rough-and-ready roving boys,
Like Rory of the Hill.

Only I did not proudly sing the patriotic anthem of Rory of the Hill, for I was devastated. I was both heartbroken and bereft over the loss of my young love. My Michael had been taken prisoner and condemned to death just as patriotic Theobald Wolfe Tone had in 1798. I felt as if I would drown in my own tears! I would desperately run to the stone pits where Michael and I had entertained happier thoughts, sink heavily onto my knees and cry for hours at a time. It was a good thing there was no one to hear me for my keening took on an animalistic sorrow. My arms and legs betrayed me. I became weak and limp with despair. I often found myself short of breath, unable to breathe, and it would take me many hours to squelch the anxiety panicking in my mind.

Eventually my parents put the puzzle pieces together and realized the missing knife from their kitchen had been used in the murders.

"How could that be?" they asked each other in disbelief. After much ardent moaning and hand clasping, they discovered my clandestine part in the violence. Devastated but furtively protecting their errant daughter, they scurried to cover up my collusion with the murders and successfully managed to conceal me within the secretive Irish underground. They were gravely concerned I would be implicated and found guilty. I was an accessory to the murders and therefore, I too, could swing from the gallows, as my brave Michael had.

Oh, how I ached with sorrow and despair! I was listless and foolish. I didn't care if I was discovered and condemned. I felt light- headed and lethargic, as if all the breath in my lungs had been syphoned and deleted from of my body. All my dreams for the future had died the same dark day Michael was tragically hung by the coiled noose. The sharp pain of losing him snarled my thoughts similar to tree roots that cross and tangle. Woven by my selfish and misguided wrath, as warp and welf, I made a childish vow to never permit myself to love again. In my buzzing mind I thought the pain of loss was too great to bear and I blamed myself for covertly accepting Michael's schemes as patriotic solutions to the Irish dilemma. Why had I smuggled that evil weapon of destruction to him? I was but a sniveling, sinful girl, craving approval from a glorious boy who suffered from noble ideals.

I slowly unraveled like a skein of yarn left for the cats to banter around and play with. I ached and I was undone!

I vaguely overheard my parents discussing the role I had vicariously played in the Phoenix Park murders and culled hesitant snatches of conversation such as, "concealed, America, and Annie." One dark night I heard my Mam crying and Da whispering, "There is blood in the hills of Ireland and the crimson stain is on our wee daughters' hands as well! She must go Margaret," Da choked out, "she must go!"

As long as I live I will never forget the desolate, gurgling sound Ma'thair made deep in the hollows of her throat after Da had made up his mind. It was a desolate cry and the sadness of the sound will forever haunt my dreams like a hoary specter in the night.

I limply let my parents construct schemes for my escape where they thought I might be safe from the forthcoming British reprisals. I was hidden away and concealed for a few dark and lean weeks as plans were made for me to travel south to the port city of Cohn, at the present time, called Queenstown, in honor of England's Queen Victoria. After I arrived there I would board a steamer bound for New York City. Once safety bestowed upon America's shores, I would proceed by steamboat to sail down the Ohio, then up the Mississippi River to Missouri and Annie's awaiting arms in St. Louis. It was all arranged and straightforward. The plan, however, did not take into account the heaviness I felt in my feet and their inability to get me there.

I had never known my Da to cry as many tears as he did on the day I was meant to leave my home and my dear family. They were all gathered around me, solemn and quiet with sorrow. Trembling, my mother pressed a small tintype photo of herself and a small silver, Celtic cross into my empty hands.

"Mo *Chuisle*," my mam soothingly whispered, "keep these tokens of mine with you at all times. When you are lonely, glance at the picture and know that I am praying and thinking of you. When you are confused and do not know what to do or where to turn, the cross will assure you that God and his angels will guide you."

I tenderly folded the photo and placed it in my pinafore pocket. I carefully hung the silver cross around my neck in an attempt to stifle the chokehold of bitter tears closing off my windpipe and my ability to speak. My sister Mary had hastily gathered together a few bundled towels and clothes, as well as some food to form my kit. She tucked a small piece of fabric into my basket kit.

"*Arragh*, take this collar of lace you once had worked on and didn't finish. Maybe you will need an example of your artwork to show to a future employer!" she hopefully implied.

My three downcast brothers collected a few coins between them, tied them up in a handkerchief and shoved them into my listless hands.

"Here Dehlia, take this bundle so you have some money to spend for necessities on the ship or when you arrive in the United States," kind Austin said while awkwardly patting the back of my hand.

"Just be sure to guard your kit closely, Thomas intoned,

"for I hear that thieves and blackguards are plentiful onboard as well as in port." My brothers had also procured the name of a gentleman, by the name of Calhoun, who was somehow related to an uncle of a neighbor of ours. He, they assured me, would be enlisted to meet me after I had crossed the Atlantic and was safe in Castle Garden, New York, my destination after the voyage. Upon my arrival, this Mr. Calhoun was instructed to book a passage for me on the steamboat to St. Louis. My parents were sure they could make contact with Annie, who would be waiting for me when I disembarked from my journey up the Mississippi River. They would mail the letter post haste and it would arrive in St. Louis before I would. It was all so simple.

Before I turned to go, my parents assured me again, that the knife used as the weapon in the killings could not be traced to our particular household. My family was safe from harm but ugly rumors had indeed circulated that a young girl from the town of Ballyhaunis had irrevocably been linked to the secret society involved in the murders committed by Michael and his gang. While my name had not been mentioned even once, I was worried there might be those who would eventually accuse and point fingers. Underground members of the Invincible Party gathered and collected the twelve dollars I would need for safe steerage passage to America. It was thought best that I put an ocean between myself and the murderous deed.

"God bless you child." Mam tearfully whispered. "May you find kindness in all that you meet," she sang out one last time.

We bravely hugged and said our last goodbyes. As I crossed over the threshold of our half-door, I turned around and took one last glimpse of my family. Their grief stricken faces mirrored mine and I choked on the phemy knot in my throat.

"Mam, Da!" I screamed out. "I can't go!" I stomped my foot down on the ground like a spoiled, little child. "I don't know if I will ever see all of you again! I can't go!"

"Nay, darlin', but you must! The good Lord will bring us all together someday. Go on with ya now!" Da quietly stressed.

With streaks of tears streaming down my cheeks and a heavy heart, I crossed to a small cluster of dark robed strangers who had volunteered to set me correctly on my journey to America. I could faintly hear my ma'thair keening in the distance, as if I was already dead. I was smuggled out of County Mayo, praying for redemption but intuitively knowing I would never walk across its' verdant land, ever again.

I reluctantly set out, traveling by foot and shuffling along with my guides and a group of itinerant workers to Claremorris, a town the distance of fifteen miles from Ballyhaunis. It seemed like it took all day to get there. At Claremorris's rail station, I produced a transportation tice'ad, a ticket previously purchased by the kind priest of our local church, and was given passage aboard a train. The lonely ride, imprisoned in the box car along with the workers, took all night long but I failed to fall asleep. I was just a powerless lass mingling among the filthy freight of cows, sheep and pigs, all of us forlornly bound for Queenstown, in County Cork.

When I arrived in port, it was the 15ᵗʰ of July, 1883, a hot and languid sort of day, and I was a dirty mess from my ride in among the tethered animals. I was fifteen, disconsolate and now all alone, inching towards a crowded steamer, embarking on a journey that would deliberately take me far away from the life I knew and the people I cherished. I looked around to try and capture a last glimpse of any *teach beag ceann tui*, a thatch roofed cottage, such as the one I had lived in but instead, everywhere I glanced my eyes were greeted with brightly painted houses of yellows, blues and pinks. It was a virtual feast of color! Then, my vision came to rest upon a most magnificent structure! I gazed in awe at St. Colman's Cathedral, the beautiful granite church and landmark our Ballyhaunis priest had advised me to locate and admire. He told me that it would be the very last thing I would see in the harbor when my ship left port. The kindly priest seemed to know what I would be feeling when he said, "Gaze wide-eyed on St. Coleman's Dehlia, for what fills the eye, fills the heart!"

St. Colman's Cathedral, overlooking Cobh

"It's a fine beauty, is it nawt?" an old man asked as he came and stood alongside of me, nudging me out of my reverie. "Don't ya see those fine, round windows at the top? If you had a bit of time to wander around inside St. Coleman's, you might catch a glimpse of Heaven when you peer through those rainbows of glass. Aye," he answered himself, "such a beautiful sight for sore eyes!"

I stared straight ahead, fearful of entering in conversation with a stranger.

"Cat got ye tongue Lass? Ahh well!" the friendly old man remarked to himself, more than to me. Nevertheless, he continued talking to fill up the empty space as we waited to scramble aboard the ship. "I suppose many an immigrant from these shores haf' dispatched donations back to Ireland, helping to build the Cathedral's stout walls! Perhaps you will send somethin' ov'r one of these days." he stated. Satisfied he was not going to get any kind of answer from me he said, "Well, it best be time to board the ship. Come on now!"

I wasn't sure of his prediction about my future monetary gratuity but I was sure many scared Irishmen, like me, had lit candles at St. Coleman's, seeking prayers for safe passage. Hmm, I thought, Mam always said no door closes without another one opening so I wrenched myself from the bloody image of my homeland and reluctantly turned around to follow the old gentleman. I tucked my head down and crossed over to the teetering wooden pier at the cove, where surely tens of thousands of people had embarked from before, most, I was sure, never to return. Was I to be among them? I earnestly prayed to God it would not be so.

Cobh, then Queenstown, c.1890s (Library of Congress)

Queenstown was the main port of emigration for the Irish. About 3 million Irish left Ireland through Queenstown. Originally was called Cobh (*pronounced "cove" until Queen Victoria visited in 1849 when the name was changed to Queenstown. It was changed back to Cobh in 1921. Cobh is in Cork Harbor)*[19]

---

[19] *maggieblanck.com*

Chapter Six

Voyage to the Unknown

I ran to catch up with the line of passengers leading toward the dock, glancing down at the thick, foul water swirling under the pilings of the weathered dock. I stumbled and stopped in my tracks, mutely staring down into the murky depths. The sun was bright and harsh, casting small flecks of simmering light on the surface of the water. I imagined the droplets winking at me and mocking my stoic reserve. I suddenly realized this waterway of the Atlantic Ocean was the liquid thread that would propel me to my future. I was loathe to follow it. Instead, I wanted to plunge myself into the dismal depths and end the turmoil hissing and rolling over and over within my mind.

Oh Michael! I screamed in my head. Why did you have to die? This life is such a nightmare! It would be so simple for me to fall into these waters, succumb to the rippling waves and loose the bonds to this wretched life!

I felt as if I were intertwined among the twin thoughts of suicide and bleakly continuing on with my miserable life. I was surprised to discover there is an almost invisible, fine line between the two worlds, a half-door, so to speak, between the light of day and the darkness of sorrow. While I was teetering on the brink of ending my anguish, I heard faint footsteps come up behind me.

"Com' on Lassie, come on now. Let's move forward. You can do it." The kind old man whispered again in my ear. I think with age he had gained other-worldly wisdom for he seemed to understand my sense of reluctance with some clarity.

"Tsk, tsk, t'will not be so bad if you just put one foot in front of the other." He confided, and so, with his hand on my elbow, guiding me forward, I took my first tentative step out of the web of confusion and voluntarily fell into the abbess of my unknown future.

Evidently the first order of business for the American owned Guion Line was to be examined for symptoms of illness and disease. Before we could even set foot upon the tread worn gangplank of the vessel, those of us emigrating were poked by curious, sharp instruments and prodded forward with intimate questions.

"State your name and place you come from," queried the stooped and harried dockside company doctor.

"Delia Fleming, from Ballyhaunis, Sir." I quietly answered back.

"Age?" he questioned.

"I will be sixteen years old next March," sounding much like the child I was.

"Let me have a look at your throat. Have you had any disease, typhus or cholera?" Not waiting for my answer, he gruffly continued asking, "Your family? Any sickness to report?"

"No sir! None." Only the act of stupidity and the crime of passion, I thought to myself as I opened my mouth wide enough so he could have a look at my tongue and feel each side of my throat, searching for enlarged and inflamed glands.

"State your intended destination and occupation in America." he growled.

"New York, then on to the city of St. Louis, Missouri, to locate and live with my oldest sister Annie, who is already living there." I hastily added. "I hope to work in a garment shop embroidering fine clothes, sir," I stammered back, unsure of why he was so brusque with me.

"Alright Miss," the doctor stated, "you may proceed on deck of the Abyssinian to receive your berth number and steerage compartment. Go on, be quick about you young lady, no time to waste staring at that ruddy, God-forsaken land behind you!"

An impatient steward, with a look of self-importance on his pock-marked mug, urgently shoved a small, folded pamphlet in my face and waved me forward.

"Here." He hissed. "Take this missy, get on with ya now! No time to waste! Read it later on, IF ya can read a'tall!"

Pushed and prodded, I reluctantly stumbled up the gangplank to take my place in line to find my berth. I hoped with all my might I would not be crammed into a six foot square berth with three others, much like the coffin emigrant ships of the hunger years in 1845. My Da said those ships were so named because they had less room for one person than a coffin! I did, however, become slightly fearful that the lumbering ship I was boarding would run aground of an iceberg! Or by chance, we might all die of fever or succumb to malnutrition onboard! The newspapers, harbingers of bad news, reported so many other people before us had! Then I realized it really didn't matter if the ship sank or not! All my dreams had already been buried with Michael, in Ireland, in a common grave, identified only by an unmarked headstone. The happy life I wanted to experience was over! Why should I care what happens to me? I felt little remorse except for the grief my family would succumb to if I perished. I had a change of heart. Since I had come this far in my rag-tag journey, I figured I might as well see what God had planned for me now. I meekly walked across the deck, hesitating often to wipe the tears gently blooming in my eyes. Suddenly a draft of wind swirled up and I caught a whiff of stale, rancid air. I was sure the telltale wind was a premonition of despair and foreboding yet to come. My nose was trying to warn me that the seams that encased my tender life were just beginning to rip and tear anew and there was absolutely nothing I could do!

As I tried to wipe off the salty tears dotting my cheeks, I stopped walking and gazed out for the last time on the colorful patchwork of fields. My eyes continued to water and droplets streamed down my face so rapidly that the last glimpse I had of Ireland was only a futile haze of smothering fog and mist. My ears caught ahold of the beautiful, chiming sound of the bells of St. Coleman's Cathedral ringing out, pealing a fond farewell to her native sons and daughters. My unwanted journey across the ocean was about to start, no matter how much I resisted.

"Down below young lady," I heard a harsh male voice bark at me, slapping me out of my reverie. "Remember, no women are allowed on deck after 9 o'clock p.m.!" I was pushed and propelled forward by the stewards who were intent on doing their job to get everyone into their cabins before the ship slipped anchor. I was rushed along with the last remaining group of immigrants, made to feel like lowly and stupid cattle shuffled down a narrow passage. The dimly lit path wound down sixteen steep feet below deck to our assigned berths in steerage. As I got closer to our destination in the hold I smelled fetid odors emanating up and choking the breath out of me. The air was stale and putrid. I took a deep breath and held my nose closed with my fingers as long as I could. As we entered the bowels of the ship the steward handed each of us steerage passengers a "donkey's breakfast," a canvas mattress stuffed with hay. As the lot of us stumbled our way along the close hallway, we were handed and procured several items, saved and recycled from past voyages. I was given a worn and thin blanket, a life preserver, which, I was told, could undoubtedly double as a pillow, and a tin pail with utensils to be used for meals. One pound of marine soap, consisting of coconut oil and lye in order to be soluble in salt water, was also included. My aching arms full, I stumbled onward, filled with anxiety and dread.

Pushed and prodded along by the callous hands of the ship's crew, I was roughly ushered into a low, dark room of rectangular sleeping compartments, lighted only by the portholes in the sides. As near as I could figure, the tiny rooms appeared at least fourteen feet long by twelve feet wide and eight feet high. I glanced up and noticed yellowed canvas strips, hung on each side of the rooms, stretched out and attached above, leaving a narrow alley in which a single person could walk to and fro but in which two people could not possibly pass between. Within each of the tiny, cramped compartments, the sleeping accommodations provided for twenty-four adults. Each person was allotted a narrow iron berth of about two feet wide. I was dismayed to discover that thin iron rods were all that separated one sleeper from another. I observed some of the dank compartments, like the one I had been directed to, were assigned to women crossing the sea by themselves, others to single men and the "private" compartments to married couples and families.

"Take a top one, why don't ya?" I heard a blaring voice behind me as I was tugging my inadequate, scratchy mattress into my assigned room compartment. "Take a top cot and then sick folks can't puke down on ya!" came the sage advice.

I furtively stole a glance around the small room to see where the noise was coming from. I spied a rather large young girl, about my same age, casually sprawled out upon an upper cot and scrutinizing me quite candidly. With not much to lose, I proceeded to heed her advice and stuffed my mattress upon an upper berth. I thanked her for her kindness while in my mind I was dreading the fact that she just might be correct in her prediction of the vitriolic spewing.

"My name is Mary. Mary Mallon, from Cookstown, in County Tyrone. I'm a-going to work as a cook in the United States as my people are all gone from this life." she abruptly stated.

"I'm pleased to meet you Mary. My name is Dehlia Fleming, from County Cork," I hastened to say, trying to remember my manners. "I must admit to being a little uneasy about the trip we're taking." I admitted. "I've never been onboard a steamship before, much less in dangerous waters."

"*Na' bac leis,* never mind Dehlia. This voyage will soon be history." Mary confidently declared.

"I sure hope you're right, Mary! I'm dreading the passage overseas. I'm so afraid of everything going wrong. What if I get seasick?"

"Ach, don't worry yourself dearie," she said. "In life, there are only two things to worry about—either you are well or you are sick.

If you are well, there is nothing to worry about, but if you are sick, there are only two things to worry about—

Either you will get well or you will die.

If you get well, there is nothing to worry about, but if you die, there are only two things to worry about—either you will go to heaven or hell.

If you go to heaven, there is nothing to worry about. And if you go to hell, you'll be so busy shaking hands with all your friends, you won't have time to worry!"[20] Mary heartily laughed, pleased with the joke she was having at my expense.

"Aye Mary, that is so true!" I chuckled. It felt good to smile for a change. Looking at her infectious, grinning face my errant, noisy thoughts began to quiet. I was soothed by her spunky charm.

---

[20] Irish proverb, *islandireland.com*

I quickly discerned Mary had a very feisty but capable way of viewing the world in which she inhabited. I was grateful for her gift of gab, her candor and much later on in the voyage, for her fiery temper.

It seemed like it took a long time waiting for the ship to leave the enormous bay at Queenstown and make preparations to sail away. Since I had only few possessions to stow away, I spent most of the time getting to know Mary and my other berth mates. I discovered there were about 246 passengers aboard, with 147 unlucky souls, such as me, in steerage. Each of us were only allowed 10 cubic feet for habitation, not much room to even turn around in! It was rumored there were 60 luckier passengers in 2nd Cabin and 46 passengers traveling in Saloon Class, where the voyage over, undoubtedly, had to be more comfortable and gracious then smothered in our Steerage Class. The talkative and seemingly informed passengers told me our Captain was Master James Price, a Welshman and Atlantic veteran, both amiable and jolly. We all agreed and considered ourselves fortunate to have a Captain so experienced guiding us. As our steamship finally left the harbor, I again heard the pealing bells from the tower of Coleman's Cathedral ring out the melancholy sound of goodbye. This time the squawking din of our ships' horn bellowed a forlorn farewell in response. For a minute there was an odd stillness all around me. Everyone onboard became silent as lambs. I was sure they were consumed in thought, anxiously filled with either joy or dread for their future. There was nothing I could do. I was trapped in my own nightmare.

I fell into an exhausted sleep that first night onboard our ship, the RMS Abyssinia, firmly clutching my mother's photo next to my heart. I knew I would miss my Da terribly but losing my mam was unimaginable! My Mother had always been the sturdy rock to ground me as well as the compass that pointed me in the right direction. I was devastated to think I was losing the one person in my life who knew me better than anyone else! In the photo my mam's strong shoulders were nestled within her wool scarf and before I drifted off to sleep, I imagined myself enclosed in her arms as firmly as the garment encircled her heart. That first night, each time I awoke with a start on my cot, wondering where and why I was there, I began humming the song, "Smaointe" for comfort. I had often overheard my Mam singing it as she did her daily chores. It helped a wee bit to steady my nerves.

Smaointe, ar an lá (A thought, on the day)
'Raibh sibh ar mo thaobh (that you were beside me)
Ag inse scéil (telling stories)
Ar an dóigh a bhí (of how things were)
Is cuimhin liom an lá (I remember the day)
Gan ghá 's gan ghruaim (carefree and happy))
Bígí liomsa (be with me always)
Lá 's oích'. (day and night)

Photo of Margaret Bridget Greely Fleming circa 1860

The next morning the lumpish Atlantic Ocean began to swell and break over the starboard rails, causing the vessel to sway and list. I awoke to the strong stench of unemptied chamber pots, brim full of urine and vomit. My stomach gurgled and growled from a lack of nutrition. I felt, between the two sensations, neither one was desirable for a spoiled and coddled young girl of fifteen to experience the first day on a swaying boat. I began to dig and scrabble around in the kit my sister had hurriedly packed for me. I located a few crumbs of dried bread, which I promptly stuffed into my mouth to stay my stomach's rumble of discontent.

My kit was woefully empty to suit my urgent needs. I thought back to the pamphlet the steward at the Queenstown harbor had hurriedly pressed into my hand as I had ambled up the gangplank. Among several statements explaining what a passenger could do while aboard the vessel, I remembered it instructing the passengers what to pack in their luggage. It stated, " Steamship rules dictated that women pack one dress, one jacket, two woolen petticoats, two sets of underclothing, two pairs of stockings, two handkerchiefs, one shawl, one pair of boots, one hat/bonnet, two towels, one brush and comb, sewing and knitting materials, and one bag/box."[21]

I noticed my Mary had carefully packed a few of those necessary articles of clothing in my kit but not all. As a poor Irish lass, I was not fortunate to have an extra dress to pack nor did I own more than one pair of worn out stockings. I still wore the dusty boots and handkerchief head scarf I had on from the night before. I smoothed the rumpled pinafore I wore over my old brown wool dress, the one Mam had repurposed from Annie's closet. I had been growing up and filling out so rapidly Mam had not had time to sew a new frock for me to wear. Under my woefully inadequate provisions I located my crumpled sample of lacework. There were my crochet hooks of different sizes, wads of thin, as well as, thick white threads and beneath it all, luckily safe and sound, the treasured coins, wrapped in the handkerchief my brothers had pressed upon me before taking my journey. Surely these coins would be worth enough to secure a few good meals as well as a comfortable train ride to St. Louis when I disembarked this horrid ship in 12 days?

Gingerly taking stock of my meager possessions, I began to look around for a decent women's lavatory for the need to

---

[21] *findingmyirish.com*

relieve myself trickled in to intrude in my thoughts. I inquired of a woman passenger and learned that the steerage lavatory was located in the "fo'ksle", or forecastle, which was situated on the upper deck of the ship, forward of the mast and within the living quarters where the sailors were housed. Embarrassed, I hurled myself past the ranks of leering sailors and stokers and through the carpenter's workshop, where the water closet was located. I was not at all pleased to notice that every time the door to the lavatory was opened, the crew would leer and make rude comments about the women they spied inside.

Within the room I quickly noticed the two wash basins in the lavatory were stingily supplied with sea water. It had a disagreeable odor that clung to my skin after washing with it. I could imagine more than one woman, after visiting the closets in the lavatory, would succumb to the foul smell by promptly vomiting and remaining seasick the rest of the voyage! After completing my first visit there I counted, as my first blessing, my already empty intestines!

I was hungry so I began a search in earnest for food and discovered that the ship provided a decent enough breakfast with bread and weak coffee, laced with some sugar and a faint hint of milk. Irish stew was included, of course, with more potatoes than meat!

At least it is something to stave off starvation for a short time. I reminded myself.

The Captain's manifesto had promised to provide three quarts of fresh water daily, per person, so I dipped up a full cupful and gladly swallowed the seemingly innocent liquid.

"Oh Holy Mother of God!" I spewed out along with the brackish water. "This water is tainted and rancid!"

"Oh aye," Mary agreed, sidling up beside me. "That dastardly drinking water has been stored in casks that, unfortunately, have not been cleaned properly. Why, it is feckin" foul! I overheard two sneaky sailors mumbling together about those same casks carrying vinegar, oil, and turpentine on previous journeys, and actually laughing about it! Why, those fellas can kiss my arse!" she fumed, her brows knit.

After observing my red face and teary eyes as a result of swallowing the indecent water, Mary intoned, "Drink the coffee dearie! Its' been heated and most of the stench boiled out!"

Wise words were never spoken, thought Dehlia. This is indeed, going to be a long and toilsome voyage!

After a tepid cup of weak coffee, Dehlia glanced around herself and roughly counted at least one hundred and forty souls in steerage, most of them a few years older than her and certainly, she thought, more self- assured. Some passengers came from different cultures and various continents but most of the people in steerage seemed to speak the Gaelic language. All of a sudden, almost as if it had been rehearsed, they each began to shout out their names in introduction and with as much gaiety as they could muster. One after another they called out, almost as if they were going to a party, "Mary! Aiden! Colleen!" until everyone had been accounted for. She met and made friends with a slightly older girl of 21, named Mary Sullivan and a delightful woman by the name of Mary

Cook, who at 30 was also considered a spinster just like Dehlia's older sister Annie. The three "Marys" and Dehlia giggled and blushed as they made tentative acquaintances with several young men onboard. She was introduced to Josh Flynn, a brawny 21 year old laborer, Charles O'Reilly, 22, a nervous, pale faced bookkeeper wearing thin glasses and 26 year old John Sullivan, a stout and hardy farmer. Josh was perhaps the most outspoken and boldest of the group. He said the words they all knew to be true, yet were afraid to utter out loud.

"We dinna know if we will ever be seein' our families again, don't we? But let's not be down in the mouth about it! Fate takes us on this journey and fate will get us there, for sure! C'mon mates, let's all sing the song *The Shores of Americay* to help cement our friendship. Come on now, put yar heart into it!"

The seven of us, newly minted in friendship and common bond, began to sing these words with as much conviction as we could muster.

"It's not for the love of gold I go, and it's not for the love of fame,

But fortune might smile on me, and I might win a name.

But yet it is for gold I go, o'er the deep and raging foam,

To build a home for my own true love on the shores of Americay.

And if I die in a foreign land, from my home and friends far away,

No kind mother's tears will flow o'er my grave on the shores of Americay."

I sadly realized our singing was the closest I would ever receive to having a wake, or a "feast of departure", the popular tradition in County Mayo of making the rounds of friends and family, wishing the emigrant advice and good luck. My eyes began to get moist and drops of tears began to run down my cheeks like rivulets of rain on a bleary windowpane. Dismally, I realized that my family was as good as dead to me. Charles, who I could tell had a wee crush on me, noticed my despondent face and handed over his handkerchief. Carefully choosing his words he quietly and poignantly said,

"There is hope from the ocean but none from the grave, Dehlia."

I stared back at him and blinked away my tears, trying to figure out if he had somehow heard the news of my involvement in the murders. Silly girl! I thought to myself. No one but my family knew about my connection. This boy just has the ability to understand sadness.

Charles added, "Horace, the Roman poet once said, 'They change their sky but not their soul who cross the ocean.'"[22]

The whole group of my new found friends were staring at me, seemingly a loss for words when one of the three Mary's broke the reverie and added to the conversation,

"Aye, *is fada an bother nach mbionn casadn ann*, it is a long road that has no turning."

"Aye, aye." They all agreed in unison, shaking their heads up and down to seal the point taken.

---

[22] Cahill, pg. 193

Right then and there, I made a vow to myself to never discuss with any of them the recent turning points in my life. The hard facts were much too dangerous and melancholy to reveal to strangers. I did not need to implicate myself or anyone else in the failed Fenian plot. As much as I wished I could confess my heart and soul to anyone kind enough and willing to listen, I decided not to. I stuffed my feelings deep within my heart, dried my eyes on Charles's proffered hankie and made a futile attempt to smile again. Perhaps by putting a brave face on the outside, I would soon feel steely resolve within. It was certainly worth a try!

At noontime, a clanging bell rang out, indicating it was dinner time. I was amazed as movable tables were rapidly lowered from the ceiling and boards placed on their rusted iron supports for seats. Each emigrant quickly gathered their own tin plate and mug and I followed suit. I prided myself on being a quick learner! Everyone scrambled for a place at the table, myself included, but I noticed the slower ones had to make do with standing in the corners of the room or sitting on the edges of their berths. Two haggard stewards sloppily started doling out a thin soup from large tin buckets, often times grabbing the proffered mugs and sloshing the hot mess into the bowls as well as on the floor! When my mug was duly filled, I tasted a rice-like liquid, spiced up with loads of pepper. I spied smallish chunks of coarse and tasteless beef floating within our containers. We were not given bread this time but offered potatoes boiled in their own jackets, which we had to fish out of the pots with our own dirty fingers! I was never good with math facts but I assume there were at least one thousand digits circling around the edges of the black kettles, at one time or another.

When our dinner was over we gathered our tin ware and climbed back up on deck, directed by the sailors to scrape our plates over the ship's side, and into Nature's garbage dump. The cook had heated a large tub with hot water and we all tentatively wound around the side of it, waiting for a chance to rinse our plates. When my turn came, I noticed the water was beginning to cool and particles of meat and potatoes were hideously swimming within the polluted tub. The glaze of greasy oil would not wash off my plate and I feared getting a disease from the contamination. My stomach violently began to lurch when I spied a coal dust-laden stoker lazily wash his face and hands in the same tub we were rinsing our dishes! I was mortified to discover my half- digested dinner was going to soon make a hasty arrival back out of my stomach! Queasy and light-headed, I turned and ran down the closest deck and straight into the thin wooden easel of an artist. Falling like a slow-motion deck of cards, the frame clacked apart and scattered the puddles of oil paint he had so carefully placed on the palette. The globs of paint landed on the canvas like missiles, splattering the portrait the artist had begun painting.

"Oh my, I'm so sorry sir!" I stammered. "It appears I have made a right *hames* of the job!"

"Hames?" he drawled, nonplussed. "You must mean a mess, dear, for surely you have!" he chuckled. "No, this painting was a mess before you bumped into it, young lady." Noticing my distress, he pompously added, "Allow me to introduce myself. I'm an artist from Southern England. I've spent the spring painting the portraits of some dowager relics, just so I can pay my rent! My name is John Marshall. Perhaps you have heard of me?" he queried.

"Ummm, nice to meet you Mr. Marshall. My name is Dehlia. I come from Ballyhaunis, Ireland."

Looking acutely at my flushed face and neck, he asked, "If you could do me the service of staying awhile here in 2nd Cabin, I would desire to paint your portrait."

"No sir, I don't think I feel well enough to sit for even five minutes." I explained.

"Ah Dehlia, you have such a beautiful complexion, so rosy pink and with such a pert nose perched upon your comely face. You are such a pretty little chit! It would do an old artist good to capture your likeness for posterity. I would love to paint and recreate your silky skin in oils instead of all my clients' wrinkled bosoms! It has been a tedious time for me these last few months. Come on girl, let's go inside and get comfortable." He smiled and crudely suggested. "I know a pretty girl such as you could be considered what the gentlemen onboard term "a saucy clergymen's daughter!" What do you say?"

Dehlia experienced a bad feeling in the pit of her stomach warning her not to trust Mr. Marshall and his ardent overtures of friendship. She was not familiar with the English term this Mr. Marshall said she was but by the manner he said it, she was sure he meant she was a woman with loose morals. Feeling her temper quicken, she swiftly located and gathered up what she could of the artists' tools of the trade, angrily threw them at him and began blindly running down the deck as her stomach began to lurch. The contents of her intestines and the nasty bile started to rise again in her throat. Clapping her hands over her mouth, she looked for a place to vomit. She spied a round, brass bowl sitting on the floor beside some deck chairs and without hesitating, Dehlia rapidly dropped to her knees and spewed the undigested potatoes into the container. It was disgusting!

"Here, here young lady." A languid male voice said as his hand magically produced a clean handkerchief from within his pocket. "Wipe your mouth on this hankie and let me help you up." Dehlia allowed the gentleman to assist her as he took her elbow and lifted her to her feet, into a shaky but standing position. Her knees were wobbly and she was sure her breath smelled rotten!

"Ta' slayda'n orm." she stated, trying not to look the young man in the face. "I am so sick. I'm sorry to have been a bother to you."

"No bother Miss, but I am certainly grateful you had the foresight to throw up in the Saloon Class spittoon rather than on our shoes!" the gentleman laughed easily. Dehlia felt her face turn crimson with embarrassment when she realized where she was. In her haste, she had become confused and had run the opposite direction from steerage! She had accidently stumbled into The Gentlemen's Smoking Room, tastefully fitted with easy chairs and lounges draped in leather. Two dapper stewards were serving wine and beer to the favored few, all of whom were staring back at her with utter disgust!

An angry young steward, with fire in his righteous eyes,

rushed over and began to push Dehlia back to the Steerage quarters where her threadbare garments truly denoted she had originated from. "Get out, get out! You don't belong in the Saloon Class!" he hissed spitefully.

"Hold on my good man." The gentleman stated quietly. "This young lady is a guest of mine, can't you see? Now be off with you, I will attend to her needs."

Dehlia noticed the steward's surprised face redden, then give her a stern look of doubt in return. He glanced back at the gentleman with narrowed, sly eyes, beginning to fathom that perhaps the gentleman wanted to have some sport with the little miss. Smiling to himself, he nevertheless, reluctantly turned to go.

Finding herself out of harm's way, Dehlia was relieved to have avoided an embarrassing departure from the room crowded with distinguished men and women, but at the moment her head hurt so badly she was afraid she might begin to vomit all over again. She did not want to cause yet another scene! She hastily inspected her surroundings and saw the room was softly and provocatively lit by electric lamps. An elegant grand piano, just like the one on a raised dias in her church, stood solemnly in the corner ready to be brought to life by trained and nimble fingers. Laid over the top of the piano was the most gorgeous green, satin shawl with silky, sienna tassels hanging off of the edges. The fabric more grand than any of the shawls her family had ever worn! There were ventilated skylights and round portholes located above and around the room, allowing precious light to illuminate the room. Tastefully appointed wood tables gracefully stood beside the sofas and chairs. On top of them were numerous books and newspapers to provide intellectual comforts for the well-being of the favored few. In awe of the handsome splendor, Dehlia's observations were interrupted when her gallant savior said,

"Come on young lady, I'll escort you back to your berth, safe and sound."

"I'm-m grateful for your help." Dehlia stammered and just managed to say with as much grace as she could muster. She was thoroughly ashamed of her worn clothing that not only pronounced her poor but assured those observing she was but a child, buttoned up tight in bodice and pinafore.

Most likely, she thought dismally, this kind gentleman and everyone here thinks I am but a young bumbling child who has run off from her family and gotten herself lost! She attempted to smooth her frizzy bangs down, knowing full well how the errant curls would spring up when she was most stressed.

"No problem at all. My name is Alec Hunt. I'm an Englishman traveling to America to visit my brother who emigrated there five years ago. I'm afraid I don't entirely understand you when you speak your native tongue but I rather find it quite charming when you use it anyway." He smiled widely and executed a formal but elegant bow. "Lean on my arm and I will take you to your family. They must surely be worried about you."

"Why thank you, kind sir." She demurred. "Unfortunately, I am traveling alone." Shyly, Dehlia glanced up at this young gentleman who had gallantly rescued her.

She observed him nod his head slightly and smile back at her. He was dressed neatly and his hair was carefully combed in place, as if he had taken the time to put his best face forward. His manner alluded confidence and poise, something she felt she mostly lacked at the moment. As they strolled back across the deck he initiated casual talk about the weather in order to make Dehlia feel comfortable within her surroundings. He was attentive and keen to make her feel like a lady. She began to warm towards this young man who was so genteel and oddly felt a sort of kinship with Mr. Hunt, even though he could have been an enemy from the shores of England.

"Enough about me, young lady. Do tell me something about yourself." He asked, seemingly interested in her story. "Where is your family? Did you run away from hearth and home? Are they wondering where you are?"

"No Sir, I'm traveling alone on this voyage with no family or companions, except for the kind people I have met among our compartments. My family still lives in Ballyhaunas and they know I am traveling to America. I am not a runaway. They have sent me abroad with their blessings. When we get to port in New York, I am meeting a gentleman by the name of Calhoun. Mr. Calhoun will be escorting me to the city of St. Louis where I think my older sister is living." Looking demurely down at her scruffy shoes, Dehlia added. "I am most thankful for your gallant friendship and would be much obliged if you could steady me and walk me to my cabin."

With a subtle facial expression of surprise, he tenderly took her elbow, steering her out of the First Class section. She gratefully let him guide her through the maze of decks and passageways. They were almost to the steerage compartments when all of a sudden he roughly pushed her up against the wall and pressed his chest into her quietly saying,

"I find you quite beautiful Dehlia! Since I saved you from an embarrassing expulsion where the likes of you should not have ventured to in the first place, how about a little kiss and some welcome exchanges of gratitude for my kindness?" Alec smirked.

"Nay Sir"! Dehlia tried to say but Alec was cutting off her windpipe so she couldn't form the words or scream for help.

"Why pretty Dehlia, I rather fancy that you are just a mere whore abroad!" Alec wickedly exclaimed. "I think I shall have to take my just reward if you won't hand it over willingly! Why would you have asked me to escort you to your berth if you didn't have something else in mind to give me?"

What have I gotten myself into? Dehlia thought to herself, eyes bulging from her lack of air. First I was accosted by a lecherous old man and now a sleazy, young scoundrel! By golly, I will not go down without a fight!

His fingers began to tighten on her arm and she saw ugly purple bruises start to flood up her veins and stain her soft flesh.

"Let go of me, you oaf! You don't know anything about me and I certainly have not asked for your affections!"

"Hmmm" he smugly whispered in her ear, "that's not the message I received! You smell like a fresh young lassie, ready for the picking. Let's see what you taste like!"

His face was close to her ear and she saw ugly sweat bloom on his upper lip with the effort of holding her still.

"Let me go, you scoundrel!" she yelled with all her might. "Unhand me you beast!" Dehlia tried to push Alec away with all her might but he was stronger. He jostled and cornered her up against the wooden wall of the deserted galley.

Her persistent yelling seemed to just egg Alec on more so. He cunningly chuckled as he began to grope with one hand down the front of her bodice, while tearing at the miniature buttons, with his other hand, pinching her and moaning with wicked, sleazy desire.

Dehlia found herself frantically scratching and tearing at the so-called "gentleman" when, all of a sudden, his whole weight was lifted off her and he was rudely pitched up against the sturdy wall of the hold! Thud! Alec screamed in agony as he hit the rigid wood and fell down hard upon his right shoulder.

"There, go back to the hole ye crawled out of!" yelled Dehlias' unlikely savior, timid Charles. The dastardly Alec began to whimper in pain while clutching onto his shoulder. Looking around he was amazed to see both Charles and Mary Malone stiffening their arms and balling up their fists. They had the look of murder in their eyes!

"Why, I'll have the lot of you scalawags thrown into the slammer!" Alec threatened.

"Aye! May the cat eat you and the devil eat the cat!" Mary Malone spit out. She shook her head, scrunched up her shoulders then carelessly tossed out, "What would you expect out of a pig but a grunt?"

All three friends watched with pleasure as the foiled lothario scurried back up the deck, tail tucked between his legs! Still clutching his sore shoulder he slunk back to the safety of the upper class quarters.

"Oh Sweet Jesus! You both came at the right time! Thank you so much! That was such a close call!" Dehlia stammered, as she frantically attempted to gather her torn bodice together. She began to cry and throw up at the same time, her nerves unsteady. "I don't understand why these men have been so rude to me Mary. What gave them the right to use me in that way?" she sobbed.

"Dehlia, no man has the right to use a woman in any way except the one she wants to let them. Most of the time men are amiss and think themselves far superior to females! They mistakenly press their own wants and desires on us. In my experience, they are rude, selfish, and don't appreciate us as persons! Phew! Stay away from disrespectful men."

"But I don't understand Mary, what kind of man can I trust to respect me? It was so much easier back in Ballyhaunis, where I knew everyone and the boys I went to school with."

"Well, take a page from **my** book of Life, and remember this; there are three kinds of men who don't understand women--young men, old men and men of middle age! Don't be so trusting of any of them from now on!" Mary reminded her. "Stay out of trouble and don't ask any man to help ye!"

"I hope you are alright now Dehlia?" Charles chimed in and cautiously asked. But instead of a vocal response, Dehlia blanched and began to vomit onto the floor with renewed vigor.

"Tch, tch!" Mary said as she swiftly ushered Dehlia away from the bewildered Charles and toward her bunk. "Lay down Dearie." She implored. "Looks like it's goin' to be a long hard haul for ye before we get to port in America."

Dehlia was ever so grateful for Mary's compassion as she tossed and turned on her cot the next few days. She became nauseous when she tried to eat and sick to her stomach from lack of nutrition. She was immured in her narrow bunk, swaying to and fro as the waves plunged against the hull of the boat. Other emigrants had brought wooden trunks, which would slide, to and fro along the floor, bashing into the walls as well as knees of the other passengers. Deep in steerage she could sense the harsh waves of the ocean buffeting the sides of the ship. She felt as if she were in Hell! Dehlia clasped the small silver cross her mother had given her and prayed for relief from sea sickness. She placed her finger on the raised ridges, tracing the circle on the crosspiece, the Celtic symbol of eternity, feverishly stroking the three lobed ends of the cross that stood for the Trinity. She had to have faith that God had a better plan for her. Surely the kinked knots and slips on the back of the tapestry of her life would straighten out in time! Surely her life would not end in misery in the middle of a deep and mighty ocean! A few gulps of tainted water was all she could manage to hold down for four days. In time she was able to swallow broth that Mary had brought her. She slowly began to feel her strength return and felt an inner resolve to get well. "*Arragh*, Mary Mother of God must be granting my prayers!" Dehlia hopefully thought to herself.

On the fifth day of the voyage, the ships' doctor had the stewards gather all the steerage class passengers together on deck.

"Come on doll," Mary Malone requested of Dehlia. "Time to get up and get poked in the arm by a sharp *sna'thaed!*" Dehlia dutifully arose, unsteady on her feet and still woozy with sea sickness. The harried stewards began to handle the steerage people roughly.

"Line up! Roll up yer sleeves!" the ill- tempered men barked out. "Hold still while the doctor gives you your shot!" they growled. The American shipping line, the Guion, required that everyone aboard the SS Abyssinian be vaccinated for smallpox before entering the port of New York City. Reluctantly, Dehlia did as she was instructed but she had little memory of it afterwards. She did notice that the doctor's lips were pursed as he inspected her pale face but nonetheless, he let her go back to steerage with only a frown and an admonition to, "Better get well quick, young lady!" With Mary's' able help, Dehlia collapsed once again onto her cot to rest. When the ship was just a few days from port in New York, Dehlia began to stir and walk about, but for safety's sake, only within the steerage compartment.

Mary warned Dehlia that she needed to be fit and able if she were to be allowed to stay in the United States. There was one more crucial health inspection to pass before locating Mr. Calhoun, the gentleman who was to meet and escort her to St. Louis.

"The medical officials at Castle Garden are rumored to be difficult to sway if they suspect any disease or illness. So *Go raibh biseach ort go luath*, get well soon!" Mary demanded. For the remainder of the voyage Dehlia prayed daily that she would not be found feeble and ordered to the hospital once she landed in port. If she was rejected from America and sent back to Ireland she would most likely be sentenced to jail for her involvement in the Fenian crimes. Truly, how much more suffering could she endure? She had lost her true love and had been forced to sail halfway across the world to escape persecution. She had suffered degradation and narrowly avoided rape. Her friend Mary Malone encouraged her to try and forget the attack she had experienced.

"Ach, don't ya know, you are goin' to start a new life soon!" Mary declared as she winked a bright eye at Dehlia. "There are three sources of new life: a woman's stomach, a hen's egg, and a wrong forgiven. Darlin' don't ya waste time mulling over all the wrongs people have done to ya. Life is for the taking!"

Perhaps Mary is right! Dehlia pondered. Forgiveness wipes the slate clean and gives us the opportunity to move forward in our lives. Surely God's promise of joy in the morning is scheduled to come for I have certainly experienced my fair share of nightmares!

Chapter Seven

A Foreign Land

Castle Garden Immigration Station, also called Castle Clinton, 1855-1890 (*nps.gov/cacl/historyculture/index.htm*)

On the day that Dehlia's ship, the Abyssinian, arrived at the New York Harbor, the shallow green water in the cove was calm and the blue sky sunny and bright. Down in steerage, Dehlia, the three Mary's, Charles, Josh and John were at last allowed to scramble on deck to behold a view of the port. Dehlia squinted and placed her hands across her eyes to shield them from the sharp rays of the sun beating down on her pale face.

"Behold, gaze upon your new homeland!" the amiable Master James Price sidled up and crooned to the group. "You will all have your land legs back again before long but probably wishing yer were still relaxing at sea, by golly! You young folk will soon have to work hard, back-breaking jobs to make a livin' in America." He stated.

"But we mean too, Sir." Josh the laborer replied. "If America will give us the possibility to make somethin' of ourselves, we WILL take the chance."

"Aye," farmer John agreed. "We er knockin' on the Golden Door of Amerikay and Opportunity is answering!"

"Pity him who makes an opinion a certainty!" the Master mumbled, more to himself than the fresh-faced youths. "Well, good luck to all of you anyway!" he said amicably as he turned away to get his ship in order for arrival.

Before Dehlia and her companions could disembark, the stewards threw a rope across the deck, marking off a passageway that only the Saloon Class and Second Cabin passengers could follow. Steerage inhabitants would have to wait their turn! Dehlia noticed a group of men gaily walking in pairs toward the gangplank. She recognized the obnoxious painter as well as the loathsome, sniveling Eric. Instead of shying away, she stared defiantly at the faces of the two selfish and narcissistic Englishmen who had tried to misuse her. As they passed by her they each turned their smug faces away from her glaring eyes! Neither of them showed any outward signs of remorse nor even a slight recollection of who she was! The thought that they could cast her aside so wantonly and with such disregard made her feel like nothing!

Forgiveness asks much of the victim! Dehlia thought to herself, mad as hell she could not somehow expose their transgressions.

The hot sun began to beat down without mercy on the detained steerage passengers as they continued to wait for their chance to leave the ship. In the late morning, an officer of the Boarding Department from Castle Garden, once called Castle Clinton in its' earlier days, came on board the vessel to inspect the Abyssinian for cleanliness. After a few hours of rigid surveillance the unyielding officer declared the ship satisfactory. With that pronouncement, several more officers from the Landing Department arrived aboard to check the emigrants' tattered luggage. Each box and kit was duly checked, labeled and set aside as the ragged and worn down passengers were sorted and placed into waiting tugs and barges to be ferried down the Hudson River and over to the main land. Their luggage was to be detained just in case they were not deemed fit to grace the American soil.

After several hours, standing about and made to feel like vermin, the ever boisterous Mary quipped,

"Oh we are surely lucky we done' hafta take a bath in the Croton water, do we?" Mary Malone sang out. "I heard that dirty emigrants used to hafta take a bath in the public bathing facilities with pure, fresh water from the Croton Aquaduct a long time ago! Maybe we need to count our lucky stars we don't get a dunkin'!"

"I don't know how much more degradation we can be shown." mumbled Dehlia to her ever-optimistic friend. "I thought we left all that behind in Ireland?"

"Aye, tis' degrading but a welcome respite from the dusty voyage over, to be sure!" Charles added, earnestly trying to lift Dehlia's spirits a bit.

Dehlia and her Irish pals were soon callously loaded into a waiting barge. Brim full of bedraggled emigrants, the overloaded boat laboriously began to move to the shore. Despite the long wait to arrive, her group of friends joyously began to say their goodbyes as they hurriedly embarked at the squat quay.

"Good luck, *beir bua agus beannacht*, best wishes!" they called out to each other, but of course, friendships and plans made while at sea were often uncertain and fleeting at best. Even though they knew deep within their souls they probably would never see each other again, they promised they would be in touch when they had secured a job and a place to live.

Josh and John each gave Dehlia a quick peck on the cheek before boldly striding into the Battery of Castle Garden. Charlie sheepishly slipped Dehlia a piece of paper. Upon it he had scribbled the name and address of the accounting firm where he was going to work at in New York City.

"Please do not hesitate to call me if you need anything." He pleaded in earnest as he gazed into her blue eyes. "May God hold you in the palm of His hand, Dehlia."

She thanked him for his kindnesses and gratefully folded the paper in two and carefully placing it in her apron pocket for safe keeping.

"*Siocha'n leat*, peace be with you Charles." she replied, eyes downcast and demure.

Noticing a romance about to bloom like a tender flower,

the three giggling Mary's began to cluck around Dehlia like hens, wishing her "God Speed and Good Luck!" However, the last hug was saved for Mary Malone, her friend and fiery cabin companion.

"Ach, Dehlia my luv', you have gained much experience on this voyage over the sea! Don't ya be too hard on yourself, 'cause experience is the name everyone gives to their mistakes."[23]

"*Rath De' ort*, Mary." Dehlia whispered in the language of Connaught. "May the grace of God be with you, my friend!"

As they embraced and clasped each other's shoulders for the last time in their young lives, Dehlia did not have a clue that in the future, all the American newspapers would in time dub her friend "Typhoid Mary", the asymptomatic carrier and New York cook, who was an innocent transporter for the bacterial infection, *Salmonella typhi*. Fiesty to the end, Mary adamantly denied she had ever been sick "a day o' her life!" Unfortunately, the outbreaks followed her until she was finally tracked down and hospitalized in 1910, never allowed to work as a cook again. Dehlia would never know her abrasive yet stalwart friend would someday die penniless and alone.

After saying goodbye to her friends of the past twelve days, Dehlia found herself pushed into a line for yet another medical exam. When her turn came, the doctor inspected the card pinned to her jacket that listed the name of the steamship she immigrated on and her passenger number, noting it all

---

[23] Quote by Oscar Wilde

down in a large, musky ledger of numerous names that had already passed before her during the day. She had heard that scores of immigrants had already crowded through Castle Garden, hundreds of immigrants processed each day, thousands each month, the same demoralizing way, forever waiting in a line without end.

She fervently hoped this stateside doctor would not find any abnormality in her. Glancing around she noticed several people slumped up against a far wall with a lapel or shirt collar marked with a chalk "Ct". Poked and prodded forward in line Dehlia found herself staring into the piercing eyes of an older man, dressed from head to toe in a frayed white garment. The churlish doctor pulled her already tired and grainy eyelids up and over a metal buttonhook, checking for the highly contagious eye disease, trachoma. Dehlia soon discovered this the most painful part of all the exams. When she attempted to pull her face away from the cold hands holding her head steady, the angry voice of the examinger barked an order for her to stop.

"Desist! Hold still! It will only hurt you more if you pull yourself away," the Doctor yelled at Dehlia. Some of his wet spittle hit her face, he was so close. The doctor was on a witch hunt to identify unhealthly passengers. He had recently found some unlucky immigrants with symptoms of the disease. The infected passengers were chalked and immediately sent to an isolation area against the far wall, the one Dehlia had glimpsed before as she had been plunged up in line. The infected would later be rounded up like cattle and quarantined on Staten Island before being deemed unhealthy and deported back across the ocean, to be condemned to revisit the conditions and reasons they had originally left their former homes. Luckily, Dehlia was not one of them. She was pronounced and deemed uninfected and instructed to stay in line until a nurse issued her a certificate of clean health.

While she waited, Dehlia also noticed some passengers marked "L" for lameness and "X" for mental illness. Luckily, she passed her physical exam but her nerves were certainly the worse for wear! She was thankful her shaking hands had not given her away and resulted in the offending "X" chalk marked upon her collar. When standing in line, she often overheard gossip that if an immigrant was to be deported for medical conditions such as tuberculosis or physical deformities, they were often at risk for committing suicide, for they realized they would be separated from their families and sent back to the world's they had previously sought to escape. It was a fate worse than Death!

Eventually Dehlia was directed to go to the Registering Department in the Rotunda, the fifth department to scrutinize her good name and person. She noticed the Rotunda was a large- roofed, circular space situated in the very center of the Battery. There she again queued up in line to wait for a multi-lingual clerk to assess her mastery of the English language, which she at least thought, was adequate enough to pass muster. When the English charged the Irish to neglect their Celtic language they were inadvertently helping emigrants to assimilate in America. After standing in line for over half an hour, Dehlia stepped up to stand in front, of yet again, another harried and overworked clerk.

"Step up, young lady!" orders were given in a demanding voice by the older male clerk. "Let me see your number. Name? Age? Married or single? What is your occupation? Come on, speak up Miss, we don't have all day now!"

Dehlia began to get a little confused with the hurried way the numerous questions were flung at her. "Can you read? Can you write?" She noticed long lines beginning to form below the signs, which read, "Cannot Read" and "Cannot Write". Hopefully, the English language she learned in grammar school would prevent her from having to conjoin with the huddled masses lining up in the "cannot line".

"Where did you come from? Where are you going in America? Is anyone going to meet you? Do you have at least thirty dollars?" he rapidly asked. "The United States don't want you if you are only going to end up in the almshouse and supported by charity!" the rude clerk spat out. Dehlia carefully stammered back her answers and convinced the man that she did indeed have enough money to pay her way from New York to St. Louis and yes, she was waiting for a United States resident to meet her here at Castle Clinton.

"Alright, alright", the clerk said briskly, "proceed to the Baggage Claim Department and pick up your luggage from the dockside. When you have done that you can go back to the Information Department in the Battery and wait. If you have someone there to pick you up, the officers will call out your name. Listen for it. Go on now girl, don't stand there wavering!"

Flustered, Dehlia rushed back to the dock where she spied her small basket of pitiful belongings nestled among a few larger boxes of immigrant luggage. When her name and number was matched up to her kit, she gathered her articles and hurried back to the large hall to wait for her neighbor's uncle, Mr. Calhoun, to collect her and whisk her away from all the confusion of Castle Garden and the immigration processing. She found an empty seat on a wooden bench, curved and well- worn from use, against the wall and gratefully sunk down upon it. The day had been confusing and arduous but Dehlia was sure it would not be long before her chaperone would come and the officials would call out her name to meet him. She had not had anything to eat since that morning and was hungry but she was too afraid to leave the empty place she had found on the bench. Surely Mr. Calhoun was now on his way to claim her and whisk her off to a train heading to St. Louis and Annie's safe keeping. She thought it best to sit tight and wait. She settled in and decided she would get a bite of food when she was safely through the imposing Battery and this formidable maze called Castle Garden.

Hour after tedious hour passed by and Dehlia still had not heard her name called out and was beginning to get worried. She wondered, had she dozed off and accidently slept through it? She scanned the faces around her of the people that joyously responded when summoned by their family or friends. They were all so happy and she envied their good luck.

Alarmingly, the murky nightfall crept in to darken the hall. Frightened of being left behind, she jumped up and began running up to various elderly gentlemen, asking, "*An feidir le heinne cuidiu liom?"* in Gaelic. "Can you help me? Are you Mr. Calhoun?" Unfortunately her frantic actions did not go unnoticed by the runners and cheats, those unsavory characters that hung around and roamed the Battery at will. "No matter how rigorous the Commissioners of Castle Garden enforced the laws of safety, prostitutes, pickpockets and other unscrupulous individuals of the lowest caliber would find a way to separate the immigrants from their goods. Unfortunately, the easiest emigrants to rob were Irish; and the majority of the emigrant runners belonged to the same race."[24]

Dehlia unwittingly identified herself as a willing victim by the fearful look in her eyes and the lilt of her brogue. The unsavory characters of ill repute who inhabited the Garden began to hover and watch from a distance, waiting for an opportunity to pilfer any coins or personal items from a young innocent, such as Dehlia, in spite of a shared Irish nationality. The runners, both men as well as a smattering of women, were ruthless in their pursuit of their treasure.

Dehlia soon discovered she was exhausted as well as scared. Many an emigrant arrived at the Castle at an importune time in their chaperones' time table. It was commonly known that Castle Garden allowed the emigrants to sleep on the floor there for a few nights in order to get their bearings. Unable to remain awake at midnight Dehlia slumped back on the empty bench, wearily closed her eyes and began to experience fitful dreams of abandonment. When

---

[24] Harper's Weekly, Vol. 11, No 78, June 26, 1958, p. 405

the soft morning beams of sunlight fell across her face, she awoke with a start, only to find her handkerchief and the precious few coins tied up in it all gone!

Oh, how foolish I was to have fallen asleep and become easy prey for pickpockets! What will I do now? she frantically thought. Then she remembered the small slip of paper Charles had written his new address on. If she could at least find it she would have a source to call for help. All was not lost! She turned her apron pockets inside out searching for it. She couldn't find it! It must have fallen out when she was scurrying around the Battery earlier in the day! Dehlia started to weep tears of self- pity for the dire situation she found herself in. I haven't been drinking but I sure am experiencing the three faults of the deed! I have a sorrowful morning, a dirty coat and if that is not enough, an empty apron pocket as well! Seeing Dehlias' shoulders heave up and down in despair, an old lady with papery thin skin stopped beside her and gently placed her velvety hand on Dehlias' bent head.

"Hello luvvy, how's' yourself?" she said in a Cockney accent. "Ow kin oi help ye?"

"Oh thank you Ma'am!" Dehlia cried out. "But I don't know what to do! I've been robbed of all my money and the person who was supposed to meet me here has not bothered to show up! I'm filthy, tired and now all my money has been stolen! What am I supposed to do now?" she asked, tears streaming down her face.

The old lady looked down at Dehlia with compassion and said, "Ow should I know? I have just arrived here as well. Ober dere is me son, dearie. Ask him."

Dehlia looked up and noticed a nicely-dressed, middle-aged gentleman briskly gathering up valises and suitcases.

"Come 'ere Raymond!" the old woman called out.

The man called Raymond scurried over to his mother and said, "Well Mum, I think we have all your baggage gathered up. Let's be quick about getting you home now! Your new room at our house is clean, ready and waiting!"

The old woman gently explained to her son about Dehlias' dilemma. Raymond stopped and set the bags down. Noticing the weeping and distraught young girl, he thought a moment and then said, "Now, surely we can figure out what you should do. After all, it is not those who can inflict the most but those who can endure the most who will conquer!" he stated, his finger whirling in the air. "Don't let a setback define you, young lady! Perhaps if you go the Forwarding Department you will find a letter waiting for you that explains why you have not been met by your person as yet. If there is no letter there, perhaps you could write one to send back to your family in Ireland?"

"Oh what a grand idea!" Dehlia agreed. "But if I need to wait for a reply where do I stay? I have no money!"

Raymond thought a moment more and then said, "There's the Ward's Island Department where you can apply for some relief from the State of New York for a time and of course, there is the Labor Exchange. The building was not damaged too much in the fire of 1876, which engulfed so much of Castle Clinton. It has plenty of space and ventilation to wait awhile. There they can set you up to find some sort of employment in New York. You can try that young lady."

"Oh yes, I can do that!" Dehlia replied. "But I don't have any money to buy a room in a boarding house while I earn my passage to St. Louis!" The kind old woman started to ask her son if they could perhaps give this young girl shelter for a while, until she could earn enough to find a flat to live in. Dehlia started to choke and cry again. Pondering how to ask her overburdened son for yet another task to fulfil the old lady saw Dehlia raise her hands to stifle the sobs. She subconsciously felt at her throat as she caressed the warm metal of her *mai'thers'* Celtic Cross! Dehlia fortunately had secured the cross under her blouse the night before she was robbed. "Oh, I can sell this! Is there a safe place to sell jewelry and other items?" she asked the man Raymond.

"Sure, look for the Exchange Brokers. If you have any gold or silver they will exchange it for United States currency. Just be sure you wear your money inside your clothes and don't look so gullible from now on!" he warned. "You're lucky to have lost only your money and not your virtue or your life, my dear. I have heard there are a gang of Irish thugs pillaging and looting the immigrants arriving here in the Castle."

"Aye, I will heed your advice, for sure!" Dehlia agreed. "I am ever so grateful for your kindness. Thank you so much!"

"Not a bother at all." he replied. "People need to stick together here in America! We all come from other lands and though our individual cultures and religions are diverse, we are all still human beings. Look for persons to help you that are honest."

"But how do you recognize an honest face?" Dehlia asked. "Who can you trust?"

"Ah, surely God will place the trustworthy before ye!" the elderly lady replied while smiling up at her son.

Shaking his head in agreement, Raymond picked up his mothers' bags and turned back around to Dehlia. He said, "Fortunately, not all the Irish immigrants are ruffians or cheats! There will probably be enough hardships for you to encounter along the way without mistrusting your own native people."

The kind old lady winked at Dehlia and reprimanded her. "Have Faith Dear, and try to remember, there are no unmixed blessings in life. The joys you occasionally experience will soften the tragedies that are sure to come." The old lady paused and wished Dehlia a traditional Irish blessing. "*Na'r lagai Dia do la'mb*, may God not weaken your hand!"

In return, Dehlia wished Raymond and his newly arrived mother good luck on their journey back to his home then turned around to ponder her first objective. She desperately needed to pawn her mother's Celtic cross for funds and then she would buy herself a good dinner. Although she didn't wish to sell her jewelry, her Da always said that a man worked better on a full stomach! Dehlia pulled her mothers' photo out of her dress pocket and held it in her hand.

"Oh *Maither*," she mumbled out loud, more to herself than anyone in general. "I am so alone and far from your sight. I hope you won't be mad that I have to sell your lovely Cross. I can just hear you saying, *Mu'ineann ga' seift*, need teaches a plan." So with a heavy heart, she slipped the photo back into her pocket and began to form a plan to start her hectic journey anew.

Chapter Eight

A New Beginning

"Indeed, this new day looks more promising than yesterday." Dehlia thought to herself. "I will heed the old lady's advice and make my parents proud of me. They taught us to be self-supporting and proud. Although I am destitute now, I will not accept charity from the State of New York! I refuse to be a simpering child anymore!"

Dehlia began a new course of action by proceeding to the Exchange Department at Castle Garden. She boldly marched up to the desk and pawned her cherished silver cross for the much needed American money. She desperately hoped she had been given the appropriate amount of currency equal to the worth of her silver, but she had no way of knowing if she had been cheated. "Anyway", she thought to herself, "it is what I needed to do and any amount of money is better than the nothing she had an hour ago!" After tucking the odd paper bills well down into her blouse, Dehlia began to forge her way across the floor of the rotunda to the area where she could buy a good bowl of hearty, steaming stew to fortify her. Sadly parting with a portion of her bartered money, she bought a bowl and gratefully swallowed it without stopping. The warmth of the broth calmed her and offered solace to her soul. After consuming the meager vegetables in the dinner, she felt dusty and grimy from sleeping on the dirty bench all night. She looked around the huge building for a washhouse to clean up in. When she located one, Dehlia marched into the open door and up to the cracked and faded mirror. She smoothed her frizzy reddish-brown hair, wiped the dirt from off her face with the clean underside of her dirty apron and made a futile attempt to straighten her rumpled clothing. She wanted to look her best when she applied at the Labor Exchange for a job. With a last glimpse of herself in the fractured mirror, Dehlia set out with new resolve, somewhat satisfied with the task at hand. She needed to locate the Battery and inquire about gainful employment. If she worked hard and saved her wages, she could seek her sister Annie's address and somehow make her way to St. Louis. Dehlia was sure it would take a while to accomplish her mission toward independence but with her newfound faith she could do anything, or at least so she hoped!

She walked to the Forwarding Department, within the dark and gloomy Battery, and inquired if there were perhaps, any letters or notes waiting for her, Dehlia Fleming, to collect? Before the clerk even turned around in answer to her query, his slumped shoulders told her there was no correspondence waiting for her.

"I suppose I could send a letter back to Ireland, even if I don't know where I will be staying?" she asked the clerk.

"Aye, you can tack the address of Castle Clinton onto your envelope if you a mind to!" he answered back. "Your folks may not know where ye be later but at least it will put their minds at ease to know you, at least, survived the trip and arrived in America."

After posting a hasty letter to her parents in Ireland to let them know she had made the voyage safely and spending a bit more of her dwindling cash on paper, an envelope and a stamp, Dehlia quickly walked to the Labor Exchange. She was confident work could be found for a strong, young fifteen year old girl such as herself! Confidently, she marched right up to the counter and announced her intentions. The older gentleman behind it leaned forward on his elbow as she approached and took in the ragamuffin look of the girl with interest. "I'm here to attain a position in America and I need to start it now!" she strongly insisted.

"Well, Miss," the man lazily replied. "We shall see what we can find you." A slight smile formed on his wrinkled and well- worn face. "Let's see here, what kind of work can you do? Have you any experience or references?" he asked her.

Dehlia quickly grabbed the partially finished collar out of her kit, awkwardly spilling out the rest of the contents, as well. "See here, I have almost finished a lace collar for a woman's dress, sir! Don't you think it fine?" Dehlia hopefully asked as she bent down to the ground to pick up an assortment of tatting needles, thread and a few gold coins.

"Yes I do young lady, but who is going to hire you to create these works of beauty? It is uncertain employment, at best. If you choose to take work of this type into your home or if you are perhaps lucky enough to find a job as a factory worker, I assure you, the length of your employment is temporary."

Dehlia stared blankly back at the man, trying to comprehend why he would want to discourage her from finding work to pay her way in the world.

"But Sir, I am a properly skilled worker, and a hard working one at that!" she declared. Shaking his head back and forth, the man behind the counter had tried to explain the situation to Dehlia in a kind way but seeing that she did not believe him, he decided to tell her the truth.

"If you are unlucky to be Irish you will most likely be turned away from most of the shops that employ seamstress's and piece workers. Why, young lady, don't you know there are multitudes of signs out there that read "NO IRISH NEED APPLY?"

"What do you mean?" Dehlia stammered as her smile fell away in dismay. "Isn't America the land of opportunity, where the streets are paved with gold and one's fortune can be made overnight? Why, the townspeople in Ballyhaunis, where I came from, have received letters from their relatives swearing to that fact"! She indignantly replied.

Chuckling to himself, the kindly gentleman replied a little more patiently. "I am afraid Miss, the only jobs open for the likes of you would be the most degrading. Here in America there is an old and often misused sentiment that continues to propagate among the ignorant, "Let Negroes be servants, and if not Negroes, let Irishmen fill their place."[25] "In fact," he added, "don't be surprised if the poor Negro calls you a "white nigger", they despise the Catholic Irish so!"

---

[25]*kinsella.org.*, Irish Immigrants in America during the 19th Century.

Dehlias' pale face began to bloom pink rashes and flush from the indignation! She was shocked to learn of this sentiment! Michael and his comrades had fought for freedom from tyranny and bigotry. Had she left one continent of hypocrites only to arrive in yet another one mired in prejudice? Swallowing a hard lump of dejection that had begun to clot and form in her throat, Dehlia pulled all five feet of herself up straight, looked the clerk in the eye and said, "Okay, then get me one of those jobs! I don't claim to be any better nor any worse than the least of them, so I will take any job you can find me!"

With a twinkle in his rheumy blue eyes, the old man carefully looked down at his listings and proceeded to describe the kind of openings that were available. "See here," he explained, "since you certainly are determined, I notice there is an opening for a chambermaid in one of the New York City hotels, not located too far from here. I suppose you can easily walk the few short blocks it takes to get there without being accosted by too many worthless pan handlers! Just be sure to go to the side door and not march up the front steps to the grand entrance, as I feel you are apt to want to do!" he chuckled. "I understand the manager is one of the few who looks upon Irish servant girls as being quite industrious and honest. Do you think you could handle that?" he asked of her.

"Oh yes SIR!" Dehlia gratefully replied. "I do and I will be cheerful and willing to work hard if I am only given the chance!" As he handed her the address and a short note of reference, the old man sighed and wished Dehlia well and good luck in her job interview. "Lord knows," he thought to himself as she turned to go, "she will most definitely need it!"

Armed with the address of a future employer, a few silver coins jingling in her pocket and a hopeful heart, Dehlia proudly strode out of the doors of Castle Garden. Unbeknownst to Dehlia, if she had waited and emigrated only one year later than she had, she would have sailed into New York harbor under the watchful eye of the newly erected Statue of Liberty, beckoning and encouraging the new arrivals to find solace within her shores.

The rigorous laws and restrictions of 1884 had made the processing of immigrants time consuming and costly. Added to the expenses incurred by draconian methods of interrogation, as well as the scandalous management of Castle Garden by its' board, the Garden gates were eventually closed down on April 18, 1890, a full six years after Dehlia emerged through its' stout doors to seek gainful employment. The change brought about a new immigration processing station in New York, the more welcoming doors of Ellis Island, through which hordes of earnest emigrants would wave in salute to the iconic statue in the harbor.

Lady Liberty declared to all,

"Give me your tired, your poor, your huddled masses yearning to breathe free,

The wretched refuse of your teeming shore.

Send these, the homeless, tempest-tossed, to me:

I lift my lamp beside the golden door."

New York City was a bustling and dirty town crouching

beneath a cloudless sky the day Dehlia emerged from the doors of the immigration center. Holding her hands over her brows and slowly adjusting her eyes to the bright sunshine, she left the darkness of the rotunda and smartly stepped foot onto the brick path that would take her to her new life. As Dehlia strode along the narrow sidewalk to the hotel, she noticed whole families of filthy men, women and children, desperately holding out their hands, groaning and asking for money to buy food or perhaps stout drink to anesthetize their bodies and souls to their current state of being.

"Dearie", one toothless hag called out as she grabbed for Dehlia's kit with long, knobby fingers, "Doncha' hav' a pittance to give a starvin' old lady?" Dehlia felt the persistent tug of the old woman's' hand and stopped to consider her plight. When she leaned in closer in order to talk to her Dehlia caught a whiff of whiskey on her breath. "Whew! No mam, I don't have extra coins to put into drink for you. I'm sorry, so sorry!" Dehlia continued to exclaim as she pulled the basket on her arm away from the pitiful wretch. There were beggars everywhere Dehlia looked. Unfortunately, most of them appeared to be Irish. As she passed a newsstand, the large, bold newspaper headlines fairly shouted at her. "The Irish fill our prisons, our poor houses….scratch a convict or a pauper, and the chances are that you tickle the skin of an Irish Catholic. Putting them on a boat and sending them home would end crime in this country."[26]

Dehlia did not pause in her journey long enough to read

---

[26] *kinsella.org.*, Irish Immigrants in America during the 19th Century.

the degrading news stories nor did she linger anymore as she passed each grasping pauper. She longed to put a few coins into each dirty, outstretched hand but she had the feeling that the few paltry coins hidden within her blouse were not nearly enough to assuage the poor's plight, for there were so many. Resolutely, she tucked her head down and stiffly marched on, desperately trying to ignore their pleas. She guessed there were probably many alm houses in New York City, most likely filled with poor Irish girls, such as herself, down on their luck and living a life of deprivation.

"I must be determined to keep my wits about me." Dehlia thought to herself. "Why, I may have grown up poor in Ireland but I remember my parents always radiated faith and hope that better days were ahead of us. I need to remember the lessons I learned sitting upon their knees!" she said to no one in general. "I must learn to be clever and survive among this den of thieves and desolate paupers on the streets of America. I have nowhere to turn to, no one to help me, so now I must help myself! Mam once told me a light heart lives longest so I am going to be positive, instead of scared, and embrace the future, whatever it may be! There is no going back to Ireland and no turning around the horrid life and events that were stitched together for me by fate. I must survive, I must go on!" She repeated her mantra over and over until she finally arrived at the address the clerk had given her.

She stared at the huge and imposing *cearno'g* rooted in from of her. The massive square building looked formidable and imposing with large granite pillars looming in front of the iron and glass doors. Dehlia dutifully checked around for the side door in which the clerk had instructed her to enter. After she located the side entrance reserved for the staff, she carefully observed the battered, old wooden door was encased with numerous locks and chains. She wondered why a hotel would want to be so unavailable to the citizens of New York City. She thought to herself, "Wouldn't a half door like my *mai'thers'* be so much more welcoming?" Dehlia knocked once, waited, then impatiently rapped twice, a bit louder! Before she could knock yet a third time, a pretty young girl opened it from the inside. Dehlia mustered a small smile and inquired if the hotel needed a chambermaid.

"Oh aye!" replied the girl. "You are just in time missy, as the maid we had yesterday has run away to get married! Do come in quickly, for this is your lucky day!" she exclaimed, plucking Dehlia by the hand from the foreboding doorframe and dragging her inside.

Dehlia allowed herself to be drawn into a large, center room while delightfully experiencing a whirl of activity buzzing all around her. Dishes were clacking as they were stacked and sorted. Friendly and chatty voices could be heard shouting to one another! There was such hustle and bustle everywhere and the familiar brogue of her island.

"At last," Dehlia mused, "a happy place to abide in!" The pretty but industrious girl leading her into the din finally turned around and introduced herself while she whisked Dehlia through the halls of the hotel.

"My names Clionna. What might yours be?"

"My name is Dehlia Fleming, from County Mayo. This

may be silly of me, but you remind me of the Clionna of the old Cork legend!" Dehlia laughed and exclaimed after watching Clionna vigorously weave and bob through the hallways. The other girls' eyes lit up and danced with mischief at the mention of the familiar tale.

"Aye," she replied with a smile, "legend has it Clionna was a wild and adventurous sort of girl, just like me!"

"Yes, but didn't the Clionna of the legend drown herself off the coast of Cork because her father didn't approve of her beloved?" Dehlia asked, hating to put a damper on the joy Clionna radiated.

"Most surely she did, but I just don't think about the sad parts of the stories!" Clionna stated as she winked her eye at Dehlia. "I choose to keep my mind on things that make me happy, for our lease on life is short!" Clionna chattered on rapidly. "I am so glad to finally meet someone from the same county as I! I am sure we will be great friends once you have settled in here. I was so afraid the next chambermaid would be English and I would be forced to work with her. I hate the English! The English might have a better life here on God's green Earth but by golly, we Irish are going to have a better life after death!" Clionna declared as she stamped her right foot into the floor for emphasis.

Dehlia giggled to find another honest friend like Mary Malone, who had shared her own likes and dislikes so early in their friendship. "Come on, be quick about ye!" Clionna pleaded when Dehlia stopped to smile and remember her friend. "The hotel staff is woefully behind on emptying the pots for the day and they are beginning to get quite potent!

Our boss would not want the paying guests to catch a whiff of their own offerings!" Clionna giggled. "I can show you the proper place to empty them after I locate a uniform for you to wear. Oh my, we are going to have so much fun!" she proclaimed as she ran off, indicating with a quick flick of her hand that Dehlia was to follow her fleeting steps. Dehlia was not so sure that scourging chamber pots of their contents would be all that much fun but having another Irish friend to do it with might lighten the load!

Chapter Nine

The Tarnished Golden Door of Opportunity

When Dehlia was lucky enough to earn a few minutes of rest from her job of emptying the noxious waste from inside the chamber pots of the boarders, she began to sort out the life she was beginning to adjust to in America. She recognized that her story was similar to many other immigrants from Europe fleeing crop failures, rising taxes, famine and political suppression but decided not to dwell on past indiscretions. Instead, she began to earnestly build a new attitude of independence in her life in America. Back in Ireland the U.S. was perceived as the land of economic opportunity and Dehlia was sure that millions of immigrants had arrived upon its burgeoning shores, carrying hopes for a brighter future than their past. Talking with Clionna, she had learned most immigrants, regardless of their country of origin, had settled near their port of their entry, and indeed, in her case, was exactly true. Dehlia was still residing only a few blocks away from Castle Garden, gratefully sharing a small room with Clionna, but in an old, battered tenement district.

"I wonder if I will ever be able to earn enough money to buy a ticket to St. Louis, where I think my sister lives?" Dehlia pondered aloud one day while dusting the stairway at the hotel with Clionna.

"Aye, if you are diligent and save your earnings, you might be able to squirrel a pittance away for rail fare. If you want to take a chance on it, many states with sparse populations offer jobs, even land for farming, to willing workers, both men and women!" Her friend stated. "If you are lucky, you might be able to snare one of those jobs, then you can go to find your relatives that have already settled into communities, like your sister, Dehlia! That is, if you can find out your sister's address."

"I know, I don't have Annie's' address and my second letter to Mam and Da has not been answered yet. Perhaps they will let me know where she is staying when they write me back?"

"Well," said Clionna, "St. Louis is a frontier city and I for one, would not venture there without knowing for sure where she is! Regardless of where one goes or not, most of us Irish are subjected to verbal abuse, stereotyping and discrimination because we are "different." She stated matter-of-factly. "I'm sure it is the same in St. Louis as it is here in New York, or even little old Chicago, the new town people say is so windy!" she mused.

"What do you mean by "different?" Dehlia asked.

"Oh my new, innocent friend, don't you know how it is here? There are mobs of northern Irish here, fightin' and waging gang war on the rest of us! Why, the policemen, who are mostly Irish as well, have a hard time separating the numbskulls! Hah, don't ya know, God is good to the Irish, but no one else is; even the Irish!"

"I didn't know." Dehlia stammered. "Why is it our countrymen continue to fight so? Back in Ireland we fought for control over our own land and lives, but here, in America, why all the angst? Isn't it true that if a man, or even a woman, as in our case, works hard and saves their money they can achieve a satisfactory life? I thought America fought against the British and won the Revolutionary War?"

"Right you are, Dehlia! We are free to make our own path here in Amerikay but there are some stumbling blocks of racism here as well."

"Stumbling blocks?"

"Hey, we have nothing to apologize for, do we?" Clionna continued. "The one thing us Irishmen have in common is our bond of brotherhood! We may lack knowledge or skills, but most of us are united, just like in Ireland. Solidarity is our strength, Dehlia, insults and intimidation by others be hanged! We help each other survive in America because this is our heritage!"

After several long months of back breaking work in the hotel, with little rest time allowed, Dehlia began to question her decision to work in the hotel.

"Clionna, is there no other place to work our fingers to the bone than the hotel?" Dehlia queried late one night. "I feel like we toil so hard at our jobs but are shown very little appreciation by the people we work for, not that I am ungrateful for the chance to work!" she quickly added. "It just seems like everyone employed here scurries around like little mice in the dark, doing their onerous chores with very few rewards. The men are not paid very much and the women, even less!"

"I know what you mean, Dehlia. I for one would love to find better employment. We work hard all day long and well into the night. This filthy job pays us just a few pennies and we are still considered the dregs of society by the people we serve! I do get weary of cleaning up after the guests' and picking their dirty clothes up off the floor!"

"Not only that," Dehlia spoke out angrily, "when we walk through the streets to our tenement in "shantytown," the air smells rank and putrid! Do the math and consider this Clionna. We each pay $3.00 a month to rent that hell-hole of an attic room, with very little ventilation or warmth to soothe us. The room is gloomy and dark. No matter how diligent we work to keep it clean, vermin are everywhere! I am in constant fear of getting sick because of them. Think of all those little children in our tenement that we see huddled on the stoops today and dead tomorrow because of the filth and the disease that is stirred up by the very brooms who attempt to wipe it clean!"

"I for one am tired of walking up all those stairs to reach our attic rooms at night, too!" Clionna declared. "I think the maid, whose place you took several months ago, had the right idea about marrying and letting her bonny husband pay the rent. Perhaps I shall soon decide which one of my beaus' shall have my hand in marriage!"

"Oh Clionna," Dehlia clucked, "surely you don't want to replace one drudge for another! Wouldn't you rather work for money at a job then do the same job for nothing in a marriage?" she asked. "I for one am NEVER going to marry! I lost my true love in Ireland and I swear, there will not be another for me!"

"Well, if you don't have designs on marrying, then how are you ever going to take care of yourself? Do you plan to feel sorry for yourself and stay an old maid all your life, nose to the grindstone instead of the blarney stone?"

"Why Clionna, there is nothing wrong with standing on my own two sturdy feet. I plan on working hard, save my money and someday start my own business selling my lacework for fashionable women to wear."

"Good luck with that! I think I shall STILL marry a handsome lad someday! After all, Irish boys here in America don't look for a fortune, only a girl with a pretty face!" Clionna added with a smirk. "Mind what my Mam used to say, "It is a lonely washing that has no man's shirt in it!"

"Well at least we have each other now, Clionna! We have enough honest work to do, a fairly well-patched roof over our head and our precious Church to attend. If we pray to God and give our thanks daily, He will provide a way for us. Like the scriptures say, *"Ask, and God will give to you. Search, and you will find. Knock, and the door will open for you."*[27]

While looking at my face, all contrite and earnest, Clionna laughed out loud, holding her elbows to her sides while she attempted to stifle the humor she saw in my pronouncement! "Ach Dehlia, remember the old wooden door downstairs you knocked on? You know dear, the door of opportunity that

---

[27] Matthew 7:7,King James Bible

lead you do this regal job of emptying chamber pots?"

Smiling at the irony, Dehlia paused, "I used to be a simple girl, Clionna. One who let others bend and shape me. But no more! I will depend on myself, with God's Will, to guide me now. Someday I will be shown the path out of here! One day my letters to my family in Ireland will be answered and they will tell me where Annie is living so I can reach her. Until then, YOU are my family here in America, so don't jump the broom with anyone yet!"

The two girls grabbed hands and pressed their foreheads together in glee. They chuckled at the thought of Clionna actually marrying any of the silly love-struck boys that flocked around her like awkward geese.

"Oh Dehlia," Clionna laughed loudly, "you remind me of stalwart Queen Medb!"

"Who's that? I don't remember ever hearing of a person by that name?"

"Queen Medb wasn't a real person, Dehlia, she's a mythical character from the story of *The Tain*. Did no one in Connaught tell you the tale of Medb, the beautiful and proud young woman who was used to getting whatever she wanted?"

"No, but I'm sure you are going to tell me!" Dehlia replied with mirth.

"Well, Medb is like you because she never questioned her right to determine her own destiny." Clionna continued. "One night, as she and her husband Ailill lie in bed, they get into an argument over which one of them is the more important and more powerful person. Ailill starts the disagreement with his seemingly passive musings that it was well for her to be married to a rich man as he. "I am thinking," says Ailill, and rather foolishly as it turns out, how much better off you are today that the day I married you."[28]

"Ach, silly man, those are fighting words for sure Clionna!"

"Yes, and Medb is somewhat astonished and just a wee bit more than a little angered at this statement. She immediately replies that it is he, Ailill, is a kept man and thus lucky to have married her!"[29]

"What happened between them? Did they kiss and make up?" Dehlia giggled.

"No, not at all! Medb was haughty and asserted her rights. She informed him SHE was the one who ruled over the province and therefore had more possessions. Naturally Ailill was not amused and the dispute eventually becomes a war between Connaught and Ulster."

"Are you comparing me to Medb with her idle threats or because she was strong-willed? Dehlia asked Clionna.

"Well, yes and no." Clionna gingerly edged. "Medb's boast was certainly not an idle one. You see, according to the old Brehon Laws, the laws of ancient Ireland, a wife is legally entitled to her own goods, independent of her husband. What she brings into her marriage remains hers. Since Medb inherited the throne of Connaught and other riches from her father and Ailill married her and lives in HER territory, it is

---

[28] *In Search of Ancient Ireland*, page 64
[29] *In Search of Ancient Ireland*, page 65

Medb who is legally responsible for him and for his debts. In other words, it is she who is in charge of his life and not the other way around!

"Oww, that must of stung his male pride!"

"To be sure, Dehlia, but now to compensate, Ailill tries to prove that he has more possessions by having the servants drag all of their possessions and belongings out of their house and separate them, to determine who had more."

"Oh what a fool eegit!" Dehlia exclaimed. "Don't you know woman always have more stuff? What happened next?"

Clionna continued, "Well of course nothing is resolved and the two sides begin to banter and war. Medb representing Connaught and Ailill, Ulster. The war is nasty with serious losses on both sides. Then the Ulster soldiers are suddenly seized by an ancient curse imposed on the men of Ulster which renders them powerless in moments of crisis." Of course, Medb wins her battle. She only reminds me of you Dehlia, because she never questioned her right to get what she needed."

"Aye Clionna, I will indeed fight for what I need and that need is to find my sister Annie. You are a blessing to me and a true friend but I want to locate the only family I have left. I know in my heart that I will never be able to return to Ireland so I am desperate to find her."

Dehlia thought it was fortunate that Clionna was a happy-go-lucky friend and never even questioned why Dehlia could not sail back to Connaught. She simply accepted the obvious and went on her merry way, unaware of Dehlia's impetuous political past.

The two girls gossiped and discussed everything except the reasons Dehlia had emigrated.

"By Jove, why don't ya look up that fella on the boat, you know, the one who saved your bacon by the name of Charles?" Clionna asked one day. "Maybe by now he has been made a partner in the firm he was going to work for? You never know!"

"I don't have his address, silly. Lord knows where he lives now! Anyway, while Charles was a sweet boy and he did indeed save me from a pig, he is much too shy and quiet for my taste."

"Ach Dehlia, shy and quiet is better than a man who tells you what to do!" I say."

"Well, I don't want any man, quiet or no! I just want to get a letter from my family telling me where Annie is living. It somehow seems funny no one knows of her whereabouts, especially since she had been so faithful about writing home when I was living there."

"I know how you must feel Dehlia. From what you have said, it seems as if your sister has been swallowed up whole like the whale in the Bible did to Jonah. I certainly hope you get an answer to your question soon, I honestly do!"

A few days later, Dehlia's wish was honored by a letter from home. In it her Da wrote,

Dearest Dehlia,

Your brother Austin is writing this letter for your Mam and me. He is better at forming the words than we are. All of us in Mayo are wishing you well and a wheelbarrow full of Irish

luck! We are glad to finally have an address in order to write you. We are also sincerely grateful America has given you some honest work to do. Just remember, Is goire cabhair De na an doras, God's help is nearer than the door.

We have received the money you have sent back to us and we are all blessed for your kindness. The saying, "a son is a son till he takes a wife, a daughter is a daughter all her life," certainly rings true with you! We appreciate the treasure you have become and miss you dearly. Your Mam often remarks how she wishes to gaze upon your sweet face and hopes you still hold dear the photo of her as well as wear her silver cross.

Your question as to Annie's address is not any easy one to answer. Our letters to the house where she was working for the good doctor have come back to us unopened. We are anxious to learn where she is and if she is well. Hopefully she will write to us and let us know where she abides. Stay where you are baby girl, and we will alert you of her location as soon as we know. We worry we have sent two of our daughters into the "lion's den", so to speak! We don't want to lose either of you and pray every day that God cares and watches over you and Annie until we all can meet again! Keep the faith, surely that glorious day will come, either on this Earth or in Heaven!

Since you left our Emerald Isles, the Representation of the People Act, or as the English call it, the Third Reform Act, has been passed, which means the country folk can now vote as well as the populace in the towns. Although the electorate has widened, we are still without much representation here in Ireland. All men paying a rental of £10 or all those holding land worth £10 now have the vote. Unfortunately, that means 40% of the men and all of the women are without the right to vote. Most of the reforms extend only to England and Scotland. Evidently we have a bit more fighting left to do.

We will write whenever we hear some news. Stay safe, Mo chroi. Everyone sends their love.
Your Da

Dehlia was overjoyed to receive a letter from home but she was distressed to find that no one knew where her sister Annie was living. She must have disappeared into that great American melting pot of Irish domestic servants, just like me, Dehlia observed. Tis but the truth, she dismally thought, we all silently serve as a "maid of all work", working 10-12 hours a day, 7 days a week, taking care of the homes and children of their employers."[30]. If solid facts were known, there isn't any work other than that for an Irishwoman. We are mere servants, fleeing poverty and famine only to be discriminated against and pushed into destitution again! We are ruining our health and life for the comfort of others. Perhaps Clionna is right, marry a man and become his property. At least we become the slave of only one man!

---

[30] Brennan-Lynch, Margaret, *The Irish Bridget: Irish Immigrant Women in Domestic Service in America, 1840-1930,* 2009

Dehlia had once found a copy of an old printed song sheet among the articles left over by one of the hotel guests and tucked it away in her bureau. She lifted it out of the dark space, unfolded it and began to re-read the words that stirred up the feelings of self- doubt she still held in her heart.

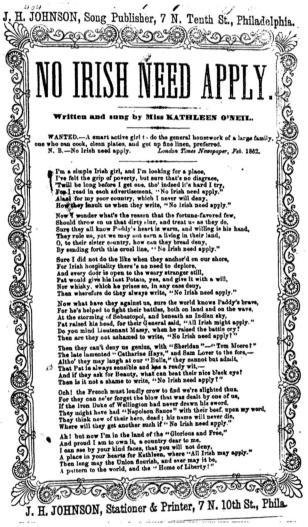

No Irish need apply. J. H. Johnson, Stationer & Printer, 7 N. 10th Street, Phila. [1862?] – Library of Congress

As she read the verses, Dehlia was curious if Annie had also encountered the same discrimination of employment in St. Louis, and if she had, how did she handle the hostility? When Annie walked along the sidewalks of her newly adopted city, did the people there jeer and call her Annie a "monkey, or imply she had ape-like features, as they did to the Irish in New York?

Above, note the portrayals of the monkey caricatures depicting the Irishmen in these 19th century sketches. Women and children were depicted in a like manner, furthermore, women were portrayed as witches. This was common practice and acceptable in the media and it was acceptable to characterize the Irish as violent and prone to alcoholism.[31]

Now, more than ever, Dehlia wished her older sister had been waiting to collect her at Castle Garden. She still wondered, now and then, why Mr. Calhoun had not arrived at Castle Garden to meet her and direct her path. Perhaps something terrible had happened to him on his way? Or perhaps this Mister Calhoun had simply been another

---

[31] *stlfire4.loudclick.net*

shiftless person, agreeing to something he had no intention of delivering. The World was full of "runners" and blackguards!

Dehlia closed her eyes for a moment before refolding the annoying, racist newspaper account. She mindfully placed it in a far back corner of her dresser drawer, out of sight and hopefully, out of mind.

"Someday," Dehlia silently vowed to herself, "I will discover on my own where Annie is and go to her!" While at work, she kept the treasured thought of triumphantly reuniting with her sister Annie, tucked like curlicues of loose batting inside her head. She scurried about her daily tasks at the hotel, ever diligent and as agreeable to her employer as she could muster.

One morning, several months later, Dehlia was on her way to the third floor to empty the fetid chamber pots left over by the last nights' hotel guests, when Clionna ran up behind her, blushing and giggling, all a flutter with girlish excitement.

"Dehlia! I have great news!" she cried. "You know I hav' been going to some of the dances the Irish Association hav' been putting on? I think I have danced with my husband, by golly! Och, he is the bonniest lad I have ever set eyes on Dehlia, with bright red hair and an' a way about him that sets my heart on fire! I am sure, if I but play my cards right, in no time I will be a missus instead of a maid!"

Dehlia just smiled and shook her head at her silly friend, knowing it was an unfortunate aspect of Irish culture that a girl was not considered an adult until she married, AND like most lasses, Clionna just wanted to get married!

"I have more good news for you as well!" Clionna pealed

out. "I was busy cleaning in a room on the first floor when a very elegant lady, dressed head to toe in black velvet, asked me if I should like a job with her mother-in-law, a Mrs. Vanderbilt, who had just lost her rich husband. Get this, the out of state family had all come into New York City to attend the funeral and were looking for a trained servant to be a "maid-of-all-work" for this Mrs. Vanderbilt, in her home on Fifth Avenue!" Whispering in conspiracy she continued, "They implied that the old widow does not want a large group of servants waiting on her in her time of mourning. Oh Dehia, with any luck I will soon be getting married, so it would be a bonny job for the likes of you! Can I give them your name?" she asked.

Dehlia paused, only a minute, from her ascent up the stairs to consider the proposition. "Oh aye Clionna, I don't have to think too long about an opportunity like that! Living in a large, bonny house, even though it is the servants' quarters, has got to be more luxurious in comparison to where I am now. Please tell them straight away I would greatly appreciate being considered for the position. Cleaning up after one old lady truly has to be better than doing this drudgery for dozens of total strangers! Aye, tell them I will apply, to be sure!"

Chapter Ten

Maria Louisa

Two long days passed by before Dehlia was granted an interview with the Vanderbilt's. Since the hotel would not allow her the next day off and insolently insisted she work her usual, long day, Dehlia quit her job with them. With a heavy heart, she remembered her Da always said a "bird in the hand was worth two in the bush" and at least she had steady work at the hotel. Now that she had "burned her bridges" she would need to secure a position as soon as possible with the Vanderbilt family. So with her nimble fingers crossed for good luck she again found herself in front of a lowly servants' door. The Vanderbilt residence was located at 640 Fifth Avenue, proudly situated between 51st and 52nd streets. The mansion was a beautiful stone-clad brownstone and appeared to be newly built. To Dehlias' eyes the structure was as imposing as the huge stone cairns in Ireland and the architecture, without a doubt, the grandest she had seen in the city as yet! Swallowing a gulp of fresh air to calm her frazzled nerves, Dehlia knocked steadily on yet another door of opportunity in her adopted land. She hoped her interview with Mrs. Vanderbilt would proceed smoothly enough so she might be offered the position. When a taciturn old maid answered the door, Dehlia nervously smiled brightly and introduced herself.

"Why hello, my name is Dehlia Fleming, just barely arrived from Ballyhaunis, Ireland and I have been sent by Mrs. Alice Vanderbilt, I believe that is a daughter-in-law of your employer, um, to apply for a position as maid of all but of course, any position would be wonderful...."

Dehlia found her insufficient words pouring out like water as she stumbled around trying to impress the dour maid with the reason for her appointment. Without so much as a smile, a friendly hello or comment, the old maid bobbed and nodded her head in such a way that implied Dehlia should follow her, immediately. She led her into the Victorian style grand hall, where multitudes of chairs and sofas, all dressed in velvets and jeweled brocades, were lined up against the rich wooden paneling. The divine furniture seemed to beckon Dehlia to comfortably sit down and gaze at all the splendor in the hall. Not allowing Dehlia the time to admire the surroundings, the maid resolutely bounded up the wide stairs to Mrs. Vanderbilt's boudoir, making sure Dehlia was winded and addled from the pace. The dour maid rapped softly on the door twice and then begrudgingly opened it for Dehlia to enter. With narrowed eyes and a pursed mouth, she sternly indicated to Dehlia that she should quietly go in, sit down on the small sofa and wait for Mrs. Vanderbilt to pause in her writing, look up and notice her. The reticent maid, with a slight smirk on her face, softly closed the door behind her as she left, leaving an air of quiet displeasure in her wake.

While patiently waiting, Dehlia observed the elderly lady,

dressed from head to toe in black silk, stiffly perched in a straight-back chair. She seemed totally preoccupied with laboriously writing a long letter, most likely something very important, Dehlia thought. She began to worry and wonder what she should say to the grand lady if and when she would eventually glance up and spy an interloper in her chambers. Should she be bold and state her request or be polite and only answer the questions Mrs. Vanderbilt was sure to ask of her? She looked around and noticed the comfortable sofa she was sitting on was tightly covered in a light-blue brocade pattern. It had tidy white lace doilies gently laid upon the arms. A nice touch, she thought. As she continued to look around and behind her, she spied something interesting directly in back of her sofa. It was a large rectangle of a serene oil painting, a vast landscape, radiant in warm and fluid tones of brown and blue. In the center of the composition were arching water fountains gently spewing water droplets onto groups of lazy people lounging about, all portrayed in forms of leisure. Ahh, Dehlia surmised, self-indulgence such as that was surely out of her reach and as unattainable to her as the fading, misty-gray mountains skillfully applied in the painting. She attentively scoured the painting, noticing how the hills in the back were a softer tone than the dark trees closest to her. Dehlia immersed herself in the calm beauty of the scene.

"I see you have noticed my favorite painting by Joseph Turner." Spoke a soft voice from across the room. Dehlia jumped up, all a flutter, and curtsied, "Oh aye mam, 'tis the most beautiful thing I have ever seen in my whole life!"

Fountain of Indolence by Joseph Turner
(*tate.org.uk/art/artworks/turner-the-fountain-of-indolence-tw0874*)

"Mine too." Mrs. Vanderbilt replied with smiling eyes. "It's called "Fountain of Indolence" and one I have long cherished among my deceased husband's art collection. You seem to have an eye for beauty, my dear! I understand you have come to solicit a position for maid in our household." Laughing slightly, Mrs. Vanderbilt continued. "My dear daughter-in-law thinks I am too distraught and feeble to know what I need at this time but I can assure you, someone young and lively would make these dreary days go by a bit faster! If you are awarded the position as my maid I promise to personally take you downstairs to my husband's art collection and introduce you to some other equally astonishing works of art. You will be amazed to find that there are at least 200 or so splendid paintings by many of the old masters."

Dehlia sucked in her breath in awe and tried to visualize

how amazing it would be to be able to stand in front of such works of beauty! The very thought of being allowed the self-indulgence and leisure time to stare at them flabbergasted her!

"But I digress, Miss," Mrs. Vanderbilt continued, "I am afraid my mind wanders and does not seem to travel along the selected path since my dear husband William passed away. Please, young lady, sit back down and let's continue to conduct this interview for maid-of-all. I am sorely in need of capable and energetic help."

Dehlia had been daydreaming about all the treasures that might exist in this mansion when she was abruptly jerked back into the present time and place with the mistresses' apology. She blushed a rosy pink, she felt from head to toe, and sunk back down on the comfortable sofa, grateful for the kindness Mrs. Vanderbilt offered her.

"Now my dear, tell me a little about your background and your employment experiences." Mrs. Vanderbilt asked. As Dehlia recounted her happy childhood and fondness for her large family she noticed Mrs. Vanderbilt quietly smiling. She was careful not to mention the clandestine reason she had been cast across the ocean and flung upon American soil. Dehlia did not want to offend the refined lady with volatile talk of resurrection and reform movements. She fervently prayed the gentle lady would not inquire why she had emigrated. She described her daily work at the hotel but explained why she wished to leave the drudgery she had to endure there and her desire and hope to better herself in her new homeland.

"And God has been my Saviour," Dehlia heard herself saying out loud, "and I have Faith that He will have me follow the plan He has laid for me."

Looking down at her folded hands in her lap, a few quiet moments stole by before Mrs. Vanderbilt glanced up at Dehlia and replied. "Yes, Miss Fleming, I too had a happy childhood, raised in a pious but poor family. You see, my parents lovingly named me Maria Louisa, two of their favorite names. My father was a clergyman of the Dutch Reformed Church. He taught me to love God first, then family, much like your parents. After we met and courted, we announced we were serious about getting married, but of course, the Commodore "believed his son was too young and too weak to marry and raise a family."[32] I well remember the conversation. "What are you going to live on?" the Commodore demanded of Billy."

"Nineteen dollars a week."

"Well, Billy, you *are* a fool, just as I always thought!"

In 1841, when I married Billy, um, Mr. Vanderbilt, he only earned a small salary of $19.00 a week and we barely had enough money to sustain us. His father, Cornelius, the Commodore, who was of the opinion my husband would never amount to anything, took pity on us and bought us a worn-out seventy acre farm on Staten Island. Included with the land was a small two-story house with an attached lean-to kitchen. Oh my," Mrs. Vanderbilt laughed, "we were so ignorant of farm life but my husband's motto was, "Maria Louisa, never attempt what you cannot do, and never to fail

---

[32] *Fortune's Children*, **page 14**

where work would win."

Smiling wistfully, she added, "To make a long but happy story short, we worked hard and turned that small acreage into 350 in cultivation. Mr. Vanderbilt and I both "possessed those Dutch Protestant virtues of industry, frugality, and sobriety."[33]

Together we raised eight children, four boys and four lovely girls. With God's help we amassed a fortune, which we like to share with Him and those in need."

As she listened to Mrs. Vanderbilt, Dehlia began to feel a warm glow of thankfulness spread throughout her body. Perhaps this was a person she could trust to give her work and shelter while she pursued tracking down her sister Annie. Perhaps Mrs. Vanderbilt was one of the blessings the old lady at Castle Clinton had assured her of. Was God leading the way?

"I am a woman of simple desires, Dehlia." Mrs. Vanderbilt added. "I rise early to attend to household duties. Most of the time I visit my children and grandchildren. I am very regular in attendance at St. Bartholomew's Church and even though my husband opened his gallery every Thursday to guests, I am not prepared to continue that routine while I am in mourning."

"Yes madam, I understand." Dehlia agreed.

"Your duties will be to rise early and attend to my daily needs as well as quietly cleaning these private rooms, where I find solace. You will carry invitations and messages to my

---

[33] *Fortune's Children*, page 16

family, as well as friends, and serve tea to us when they arrive to visit. Since I do not wish to have many servants around, I am afraid you will most likely be on call all the time." Mrs. Vanderbilt reluctantly added, "And you probably will not have time to attend the dances and gaieties that young girls certainly like to delight in."

"Oh 'tis alright," Dehlia agreed, "I don't wish to go to those dances and I don't want to meet any boys! I just want to learn how to blend into America and develop good manners and poise!"

"Well I can certainly help you with that young lady. I must admit that it puzzles me to think you don't desire meeting up with other young people your age but, I suppose you'll have our art collection to hold your interest. I understand you Irish have a saying, "what fills the eye fills the heart!"

"Oh yes Mam, I am curious to learn all I can! If I could only discover how an artist can translate Gods beauty onto a canvas. That surely would be a revelation!"

"Well then," Mrs. Vanderbilt firmly stated, "That is it! Let me ring for Miss Elliot, my English housemaid, who showed you to my boudoir. She can take you to the servant quarters and assign you a room. You can start at 5:30 tomorrow morning when I first ring for you. Your working day will end about ten in the evening when your chores and errands are finished. I will pay you $3.25 per week to start off and after six weeks, if you work out well for me, I will raise it to $3.75. You will have your room and board here, as well as all your meals. On Sunday, your day off, you will be able to attend churches services. I will certainly understand if you wish to continue going to your Catholic Church but please consider the fact that you are welcome to come with me to our congregation, as well. Does that sound agreeable to you, my dear?"

"Oh yes! It does indeed!" Dehlia countered. "That is more than generous and I am anxious to begin right away!"

"Thank you Dehlia, I should think we will get along famously."

With that said, Mrs. Vanderbilt looked back down at her writing and Miss Elliot, who had been listening and silently hovering behind the door, came in the room to reclaim her. Stiffly, the sour maid beckoned Dehlia to follow her down the narrow, back staircase that darkly curved into the servants' quarters. Dehlia was trying so hard to squelch the happy feeling of satisfaction in procuring the position. Oh how she wanted to dance with anticipation! However, she reminded herself, this was a house in mourning and she would need to curtail her excitement out of respect for the dead. Oh there will be time for smiles and chuckles in due time, she thought as she censored herself with a furtive glance at the English maid leading her to her appointed room. When Miss Elliot indicated which of the servants rooms were to be Dehlias', she poked her dour face into Dehlias' youthful one and commenced barking orders.

"I will check our cleaning rota promptly and let you know just what activities you will be required to complete this evening."

"Oh no, I beg your pardon Miss Elliot, but Mrs. Vanderbilt stated that I should rest and not begin my chores until the 'morrow! Surely you are mistaken?"

"Hmmph!" the old maid stiffened with indignation. "Like I said, I will check and let you know!" and with that, turned briskly and headed back down the narrow stairs.

Ahh, I think I have made an enemy of that one! Dehlia thought to herself as she glided into her room. Gluais faicill each e cupan la'n. Miss Elliot had best go carefully with a full cup!

As she unpacked her extra dress and well- worn pinafore and hung them on the wooden pegs attached to the wall in her room, Dehlia counted her many blessings. With gainful employment in a wealthy, private home as elegant as this one, a kind mistress to work for, and a promised increase in salary she would be able to save more money to send back home to her family. She would be able to add a few more coins to her Sunday tithe, as well as save for her eventual trip to St. Louis. Even though she had to work six long days a week here, she was sure she could still find spare time to crochet some dainty lace collars or doilies in the hopes of building an inventory of work for future references. "It is just too bad crochet work is so slow and painstaking." Dehlia thought to herself. "It takes time to build up the patterns of roses and leaves so they look like they could certainly bloom! Nonetheless, I will be much too busy crocheting at night and working during the day to weep for the loss of my family or mourn my sweet Michael anymore! In time, perhaps Mrs. Vanderbilt will instruct me in the manners and methods befitting a lady who owns a fashionable shop selling lace? Perhaps my joy will truly come in the morning? Oh Jesus, Glory be Thy name!" she fervently prayed.

Early the next day, before the sun was up, a groggy Dehlia was awoken by an unrelenting Miss Elliot, who began instructing her in the routine Mrs. Vanderbilt had discussed the previous day. Dehlia went about her business as diligently and efficiently as possible. Even the taciturn Miss Elliot seemed a tad impressed. The long working days faded into many boring nights until one morning, a few weeks later, Dehlia noticed a headline emblazoned on the newspaper that she had been using to scoop up the ashes from one of the fireplaces. She carefully deposited the ashes into the ash bin and unfolded the black and white paper laid out before her. The December 26, 1885 issue of *The New York Times* reported a series of murders, referred to as "**The Servant Girl Murders.**" Dehlia gasped out loud when she read that the "murders were committed by some cunning madman, who is insane on the subject of killing women."

"I see you can read an English speaking newspaper headline, can't ye now?" the voice of Miss Elliot, who had crept in behind her, snidely implied.

Startled from being lost in thought and reading the text, Dehlia hastily dropped the newspaper back onto the floor from fright. "Oh aye, I can!" she stammered back, feeling foolish for taking the time away from her prescribed duties.

"Well then, you might just mind your pretty neck and stay away from Austin, Texas where the victims were attacked and mutilated!" Miss Elliot smirked. "Don't be getting any fancy, mucky-muck ideas about being better than the rest of us just because Mrs. Vanderbilt seems to have taken a liking to ye now! All you high and mighty "Bridgets" from Ireland think you're better than us." She spat out. "Perhaps there is a killer waiting to grab you, drag you outside and stab the life out of ya, right here in good old New York!" she chuckled like an old crow. "Why, you had better keep your pretty feet planted firmly in this brownstone, for safety sakes!"

"No Madam, I don't think I will be going anywhere outside this mansion for now, thank you very much!"

"Well, I suppose those darkies in Texas had it comin' alright! Six of the eight victims were right off the slave ship, Missy!" she venomously spewed out.

After the hypocritical old maid turned and left the room as silently as she had entered it, Dehlia reached back down, picked the ash laden pages of the newspaper up off the floor and continued reading the horrific story in the *Times*. It read, "according to the *Texas Monthly*, seven females (five black, two white), and one black male were murdered. All of the victims were attacked indoors while asleep in their beds. Five of the female victims were then dragged, unconscious but still alive, raped and killed outdoors. Three of the female victims were severely mutilated while outdoors."

"Oh my," Dehlia exclaimed aloud, "what a bloody, gruesome scene that must have been! She continued reading, "According to *Texas Monthly*, all of the victims were posed in a similar manner. Six of the murdered female victims had a "sharp object" inserted into their ears.

"Arrah! There is murder and mayhem everywhere!" Dehlia darkly mused. "I suppose it starts when someone takes a disliking to another person for some overlooked slight, much as that old biddy Elliot seems to have taken with me!

And the vitriol she spews about her! Mam taught me that the color of ones' skin is not an indication of the depth of their soul. Why, Clionna would have laughed and declared her an 'English witch!' Da would say, 'put silk on a goat and it is still a goat', but I best be minding my manners and stay out of her way as much as possible," Dehlia thought to herself. "Anyway, the old maid, being English, isn't aware the Irish name Dehlia is a shortened nickname for Bridget. If the old drudge could look farther beyond her snooty nose, she would see that I am indeed proud of the name distinction and my Celtic nationality! Harrumph! High and mighty indeed!"

As the days passed by, Miss Elliot became even more morose and forbidding toward Dehlia, criticizing her cleaning and constantly attempting to convert her to the Protestant faith. Dehlia was aware "some Protestant employers did not consider Catholics to be Christians and thus tried to convert their Irish domestics to Protestantism."[34] "I am lucky," Dehlia thoughtfully considered, "that Mrs. Vanderbilt did not share these same missionary opinions."

Even though the mistress of the house was quiet and reserved, she nevertheless remembered her promise to help Dehlia become a cultured domestic as well as a trained servant. Mrs. Vanderbilt often took a few minutes out of her day to instruct Dehlia, her constant companion, in etiquette and the rules universally accepted by good society.

Dehlia was smart and aptly learned decorum in how to

[34] *Ubiquitous Bridget: Irish Immigrant Women in Service in America, 1840-1930*, Lynch-Brennan, Margaret, page 336

make introductions among ladies and gentlemen. She was groomed in the rigid politeness of the day but occasionally faltered over the confusion of the significations of visiting cards. She encountered daily nuisances with the visitors that insisted on seeing Mrs. Vanderbilt, ignoring her season of mourning and only desiring to ask for favors of her hospitality.

"Why on God's green earth do callers twist and turn their calling cards this way and that!" Dehlia huffed under her breath. "Seems like they should just state what they want right off and not engage in these little shenanigans! Let's see if I have this correct. If a visitor's card is turned to the upper right corner it means they have come for a visit, and turned to the lower right, adieu. If the upper left corner is turned it means congratulations, but really," Dehlia thought, "in this household, right now, visiting cards should only be turned to the lower left corner, meaning condolences. Poor Mrs. Vanderbilt should be allowed ample time to grieve the love of her life! I wish these self-serving leeches would go suck the blood from someone else for a change!"

One late January afternoon in 1886, Mrs. Vanderbilt called Dehlia to her suite.

"My dear," she began, "I have just received this publication in the mail and have had the opportunity to study it in some detail. I believe if you were to read it over and take it to heart, it would be of great help to you in furthering your refinement of manners." Dehlia extended her hand to grasp the literature while carefully glimpsing title. It read, GOULDS BLUE BOOK FOR THE CITY OF ST. LOUIS., VOL. IV.

"Thank you," she replied. "I will go over it willingly when I have time, my lady."

Mrs. Vanderbilt continued, "While I do not think that the small prairie city of St. Louis is a mecca of social graces like our New York, but I do believe some importance can be gleaned from between the books' covers."

"Yes mam. I will be sure to read it from front to back." Gratefully, Dehlia tucked the slender pamphlet under her arms and scurried away to finish her dusting in the room. In all the busyness of her daily job, she forgot about reading it until a few days later when she spied it where she had shelved it. The pamphlet was almost hidden from view, lying beneath the tangled bobbins of lace thread and samples of the ladies' collars she had been so hard at work on. That very night she picked the booklet up and casually started leafing through the pages. She read the first page, "Decorum," says a French writer, "is nothing less than the respect of oneself and others brought to bear upon every circumstance of life. In all relations, whether social or domestic, anything approaching coarseness, undue familiarity or levity of conduct, is prolific of evil."

"Hmm," thought Dehlia, "I think I can be considered elegant since Life has certainly brought undue circumstances into my world, and, I have survived with dignity and decorum!" Giggling to herself, she continued reading, "In introductions among ladies, it is the younger lady who is introduced to the elder." "Why," Dehlia thought, "that's just good manners and my *mai'ther* taught me those!" She eagerly read on, "Guests should arrive at dinner parties five or ten minutes before the hour named in the invitation." Hah, I don't think that means me! I'm usually helping out in the kitchen, not arriving at the front door like a grand lady! With only half a mind at attention, Dehlia glanced down the pages and casually perused the advertisements, "P.C. MURPHY, MANUFACTURER OF ALL KINDS OF TRUNKS AND VALISES, ST. LOUIS DAIRY COMPANY, SCRUGGS, VANDERVOORT & BARNEY DRY GOODS COMPANY, 417 TO 425 NORTH FOURTH STREET, A.P. ERKER, OPTICIAN, ADAM FLICKINGER, D.D.S." Her eyes stopped on the last advertisement for the dentist. Something was very familiar about the name of Flickinger. Where had she heard of it before? Of course! That was the last name of the little boy her sister Annie had wrote to her about a few years ago! Henry Flickinger, and Annie had said that his father was a Doctor of Dentistry, in St. Louis! Could it be one and the same? Would she be able to find the whereabouts of her sister from this doctor? She scanned the paper for the address. Let's see, his office is at No. 708 Pine Street and his residence is 2802 Caroline Street. The numbers and street names meant nothing to Dehlia but she was sure Mrs. Vanderbilt would help her uncover the mystery of her sisters' disappearance. She could not wait until the next morning to beg for her employers' help. *"Meileann muilte De' go mall ach meileann said go mi'n,* the mills of God grind slowly but they grind finely!" Dehlia confidently thought to herself.

Chapter Eleven

The Promise of a New Day

Dehlia was up at the crack of dawn and hustling through her daily chores as she began to formulate a plan on how to ask Mrs. Vanderbilt to help her locate her sister Annie in St. Louis. One of her last chores of the morning was to dust the heavily gilded and wood laden frames of the late Mr. Vanderbilt's art collection and keep the paintings leveled on the walls, a constant and tedious job. However, Dehlia was reverent enough to be in awe of the classical art hung before her. After all, she thought to herself, how many immigrant Irish maids were fortunate enough to have the opportunity to stand and gaze at Eugene Delacrois' *Sultan of Morocco with His Officers and Guard of Honor,* with its cerulean sky and jauntily placed red umbrella tilted in the Sultan's hand, much less study and wonder at the perspective of the stairway in the *Louis XIV and the Grand Conde'* by Jean-Leon Gerome?

She was just contemplating the bold and vivid brushstrokes when Miss Elliot snuck up behind her and crooned, "Wasting your time, Miss Bridget, instead of doing your work are ye? I bet the Missus would not be pleased to see you standing there gawking at her art collection, worth more money than you will ever see in your lifetime, I guarantee!"

"Oh", Dehlia said with a start. "I'm not wasting time Miss Elliot, only taking a few moments to admire the beauty of the artwork."

"Tsk, tsk," the sour old lady replied, "time is money and you are indeed squandering her Lady's fortune, if I do say so myself!"

"Now, now there Miss Elliot," Mrs. Vanderbilt quietly intruded on the conversation she overhead as she was passing by the room. "I couldn't help witnessing your wrath directed toward our little maid but I must inform you, she is doing an excellent job in this household. I would warn you to please hold your tongue and the next time, if you observe any discrepancies you should report them to me, not handle them yourself. You are excused, Miss Elliot." With a stiff back and a churlish manner, the Englishwoman left the room in a subtle but audible huff. Mrs. Vanderbilt turned back to Dehlia and said, "I'm terribly sorry Miss Elliot is giving you such a hard time of it but she really is a valued employee albeit an outspoken one at times. She is just a bitter old maid and probably jealous of your youth and vitality."

"And I am terribly sorry if I was wasting time staring at the paintings, please forgive me?" Dehlia begged.

Mrs. Vanderbilt serenely gazed up at her husbands' mounted treasures and remarked, "I don't know what I am going to do with these beauties, Dehlia. My daughter Margaret Louise has asked me to close the mansion and come live with her. I am beginning to consider the option very seriously. It would be wonderful to be around the grandchildren more often than I am now, and living this solitary life, in this huge home without my husband, is so depressing."

Dehlia blinked and felt as though she had swallowed a lump in her throat. Would Mrs. Vanderbilt want Dehlia to follow her to the countryside where her daughter lived or would she instead ask Dehlia to seek employment elsewhere? She seized the opportune moment to ask Mrs. Vanderbilt to help her locate her sister. Dehlia related the surprise of finding the dentist's name in Gould's Book of Etiquette.

"Mrs. Vanderbilt, mam, surely this is a lucky coincidence, would you not think so?" Dehlia implored. Mrs. Vanderbilt just smiled and with kindly eyes, promised she would indeed, have her solicitor look into it.

"Dehlia, only time will tell if this is a gift from God, or simply a wild goose chase! I fear, my dear, you will get your hopes up, so be cautious and let my solicitor leave no stone unturned." Stating what Dehlia knew to be true, Mrs. Vanderbilt gracefully swept from the room.

The next few months passed by, slowly as usual, with Dehlia busy dusting, waiting on Mrs. Vanderbilt and trying hard to ignore Miss Elliot's haughty manner. It was difficult for her to contain her curiosity and refrain from asking her employer of any news from the solicitor. Patience, she thought to herself. I must remember that little by little, the bird builds her nest. I must have faith and pray that Saint Anthony, our patron saint of lost things, will help us find Annie in due time. In New York, the icy month of January evolved into a bitter, cold February, which begat the blustery months of March and April. Then, one fine day in early spring, Mrs. Vanderbilt summoned Dehlia into her rooms for a talk.

"My dear, I believe we have a bit of good news! My solicitor thinks the sister you are looking for is indeed in St. Louis and going by the name of Annie Bohn. She lives with her husband Frank, in what the local people call "Dogtown," a working class district off of Tamm's Avenue. He has given me the address in which to reach her. With that small tidbit of welcome news Dehlia could not contain her excitement and started to jump up and down. She began to dream of reuniting with her sister and how excited her parents would be when they found out she was safe and sound!

"But Dehlia, I must caution you, try not to get your expectations up too high. This might very well be the wild goose chase I told you about a few months ago and come to naught."

"Oh thank you, thank you so much Mam!" Dehlia cried undaunted. Mrs. Vanderbilt offered the small slip of paper with the name and address on it to Dehlia and told her she was excused.

"Go compose your letter, post it immediately and notify me when you receive an answer. If this lady is indeed your sister, I will help you book passage to St. Louis so you may be reunited with your family. Good luck my dear."

Dizzy with delight, Dehlia ran all the way up the dark and narrow servant stairs to her room at the top of the landing. She pulled out her stationary and began writing her letter, as fast as her tiny fingers could fly! She had so many questions to ask but was afraid to insert too much information into her letter, after all, this woman might not be her sister. It very well could be a stranger to whom her letter of introduction was addressed to. After re-reading her fairly stiff and formal note over a few times, she hurried downstairs to post the envelope in with the days' mail.

"Wait and see, wait and see, and pray, pray, pray!" she sang to herself.

Dehlia only had to wait a few weeks until a return letter arrived from St. Louis with the familiar slanted writing of her beloved sister Annie. She quickly tore off the side of the envelope and anxiously began reading the long awaited words she had been praying for.

May 1, 1886
My dear, dear Dehlia,
Cead Mile Failte! A hundred thousand welcomes! Oh, so much time has passed since I last gazed upon your bonny freckled face! I cried tears of joy for days when I discovered your inquiry in our mail box. I am so distressed that it has been difficult for you to locate me and I understand the formality of your letter. Life has had its' ups and downs but I sense that we are going to be rewarded for our diligence soon.

I do not remember when we last communicated by letter but let me fill you in on what I recall. As you know, when I arrived in the States, I was incredibly lucky to have a proper job as a nanny to a darling, wee boy. The father, who lost his wife and the mother of the child, while traveling in Europe, brought me to Missouri and put me in charge of dear Henry. For a time, I believe my letters were still sent to you and our family in Ireland.

I cannot believe your employer tracked me down through his advertisement in the newspaper!

Anyway, to make a very long story short, after the cholera that ravaged the city, and took my little Henry as its' last innocent victim, the kind Doctor closed his dental office and committed himself to a sanitarium while he grieved. I was out of a job for a while, and completely destitute until I happen-chanced upon a grand lady by the name of Susan Blow. Oh my darling! I get ahead of myself sometimes! Let me explain anew.

One day I was stumbling along the cobbled brick streets near the Mississippi River, contemplating my dire and unemployed future, when a horse and carriage ran over me. The reckless driver was in a hurry to catch a steamboat to New Orleans and said he didn't see me! I must have hit my head on the hard bricks as I do not recollect what happened next. All I know is that I ended up in hospital, unsure of who I was and what my name was. This was when I lost contact with all my loved ones. So sad!

While I was convalescing in hospital, a kind lady in the bed next to me began a conversation and we discovered we both had a tender heart for young children. The lady said her name was Miss Susan Blow. She declared she was in fragile health at the time and was recovering from fatigue and poor mental health. She stated that she was an educator and had spent many years promoting the pedagogy, the educational doctrine, of a German professor by the name of Friedrich Froebel. Mr. Froebel believed that young children learn best by playing with objects, such as balls and blocks, in pursuit of language, math and science skills. I remember Miss Blow said, "If we can make children love intellectual effort, we shall prolong habits of study beyond school years."[35]

Miss Blow told me she was going to retire from public service and

---

[35] *The State Historical Society of Missouri-Susan Blow, shs.umsystem.edu*

attempt to write some theories about her "kindergarten" work, or the "child's garden", as she called it. She asked if I would like a job in one of the schools. Of course, I sprang at the opportunity to work with young children again and so, after a brief period of recovery, I started work for her, but under an alias, since I could not recollect my own name. Dehlia, it was a long time until the cloud of darkness became fog and then lifted into light. It took months to regain my memory and by that time I had lost all contact with you and our family in Ireland.

I spent many happy hours working in St. Louis kindergartens. I will tell you more about my work when you arrive here. Not so long ago I met a wonderful and kind man by the name of Frank Bohn, a German immigrant, who handily wooed me. Can you imagine that? Your old spinster of a sister wooed! We had been wed only a few months when I received your letter. Your letter gave my old memory a jog and I remember so much more of my life now! Oh gracious Dehlia! To be able to see you and wrap you in my arms once again! I have included our address and directions to our home in Cheltenham." Mo chuise, please come right away and live with us. Cronaim thu, I miss you!

Annie

P.S. Please do me a favor and write Mam and Da. Let them know I am well and you are on your way to St. Louis.

As soon as Dehlia read her long lost sister's letter, she immediately wrote a long letter to her parents in Ireland and began making preparations to travel to St. Louis, thankfully, with Mrs. Vanderbilt's help and guidance. She often thought to herself, *Muineann ga seift*, need teaches a plan and with angels such as Mrs. Vanderbilt hovering over her and helping, the plan to be reunited with Annie was made possible. Dehlia was anxious to travel as soon as the arrangements could be made. Mrs. Vanderbilt quickly bought her a ticket to her destination.

"Dehlia," Mrs. Vanderbilt softly said, "here is a ticket to travel by steamboat to St. Louis. Water transportation is still the most efficient mode of travel these days."

"Thank you so much! You have been more than kind." Dehlia blurted out.

"Now listen to these directions carefully." Mrs. Vanderbilt began again. "You will embark on your journey at the Erie Canal, right here in New York City. It is really quite the easiest way to circumvent the Appalachian Mountains. Next, you will get off at Buffalo, New York, clear across the state, and travel by rail across the state of Ohio to the Ohio River. Once there, you will board a steamboat that will take you down the river to a town by the name of Cairo, Illinois. When you arrive there, the workmen will transfer goods to the dock but you should remain on the steamboat until the deed is done. Don't take a chance on wandering off in a strange town, especially one so far from proper civilization. The Steamboat will ascend the mighty Mississippi River to your destination of St. Louis. Do you understand, my dear?" she queried.

"Oh yes mam! I do indeed and I want to thank you from the bottom of my heart for your many kindnesses!" Dehlia exclaimed with a tearful catch in her voice. "You have instructed me in many ways and I feel much more competent since I came to work for you. I will never forget you. I will say a prayer for you to Saint Peter each day for long life, as well as a prayer for your happiness while living at your daughter's house."

"You have been a blessing too, Dehlia. You have always been pleasant and helpful and often I think on you as a daughter. I believe the Irish have a blessing that says, may the road rise with you! Go with my fondest wishes for a future full of promise and reward. May God make you prosperous!" she called out as Dehlia turned to go.

Hmm, thought Dehlia, I remember my *Mai'ther* saying the same thing to my Da when he left for work each day. Perhaps God created all mothers' hearts the same, regardless of race or religion. They always seem to hope for the best and wish us well on our chosen paths.

Chapter Twelve

St. Louis Bound

In the merry month of May, 1886, as Dehlia commenced her trek across the states of New York and Ohio, she often discovered her fingers lingering near her neck where the silver Celtic cross her *mai'ther* had given her had once hung. She could not believe she was, at long last, on her way to Annie's waiting arms but oh, how she wished she still had that small talisman of her mother's love to speed her on her way! She felt she needed it to give her the courage to travel down the mighty Ohio River. When Dehlia had the steamboat ticket Mrs. Vanderbilt had previously bought for her duly stamped and approved, she was told by the ticket agent that the swift Ohio River had been named the "Great River" by the Seneca Indians, who had first traversed it. Shuddering with regret, she prayed and hoped for a swifter, safer journey down the Ohio and up the muddy Mississippi than the one she encountered crossing the ocean just a few years ago.

What if the steamboat should collide with a snarly snag in the water and have a hole ripped into the hull? She worried. Could a large ship still navigate in shallow waters with vicious sandbars waiting to sink them? What about the hazards of boiler explosions that scald and maim innocent travelers? Dehlia had heard of many disasters occurring on the rivers. When Dehlia arrived at the apex of the Ohio River, she took a curious look at *The City of St. Louis,* the boat she would soon be boarding. Black billows of smoke were belching from the boiler and the wood timbers of its' Gothic construction appeared to look like a brittle construction of bones, as if the boat were yet a bug with its' skeleton on the outside. She noticed that there were about six levels or decks that were beginning to fill up with passengers. Fear and dread of repeating another harrowing passage kept her from stepping aboard.

City of St. Louis Anchor Line steamboat, before 1903.
Published by St. Louis News Company, St. Louis,
Missouri.

"Hurry up, Miss," a kindly conductor interrupted her reverie. "Let us take a look at yer ticket now, and see where we need to put ya."

She reluctantly offered her pre-purchased ticket from Mrs. Vanderbilt for the elderly officer to check over.

"Oh aye, Miss, this ticket says yer to take a seat on the second deck, in the Gallery, a fine ride to be sure! Enjoy your ride down the Ohio River to Cairo, the city they call the "Egypt" of Illinois!" he said as he winked. "When you get there, be prepared to stop for a few hours while goods are transferred on and off the boat. Do not disembark young lady, for she will be moving back up the mighty Mississippi River to St. Louie, your final destination."

"Thank you Sir. I will remember your advice." Mrs. Vanderbilt had bought her a more expensive ticket than she would have purchased for herself. She was grateful to have access to the open spaces around her and not feel like an animal penned in the steerage compartment as she had experienced crossing the Atlantic. Sure, she thought to herself, it is truly different plying the whirling river than the wide blue ocean, but while I am not ashamed of my humble roots, it is far better to have a little money to oil the wheels of transportation! She shyly glanced around at the numerous ladies and gentlemen strolling upon the deck. They were fitted in fine, elegant clothing. The men sported top hats and gloves and the ladies swished to and fro in swirling gowns of taffeta and lace.

"Goodness, I am so thankful Mrs. Vanderbilt took pity on me and added this beautiful traveling cloak to my wardrobe!" Dehlia ran her fingers down the sides of her cloak, feeling the richness of the silver-gray "vigogne" or what her former employer said was fine wool from a small animal called the vicuna. The lovely trim down the front of the cap-sleeve, as well as the back of the skirt sported a contrasting "passementerie". This braided trim was a darker shade of gray velvet that loaned the garment an elegance that Dehlia was not accustomed to. Unbeknownst to her fellow passengers, beneath her traveling clothes were the simple dresses of a chambermaid but enclosed in her finery, Dehlia felt she passed muster among the most fashionable guests. With new found confidence she proceeded up the deck and into the room the officer had called the Gallery. She noticed there were plenty of places left to sit. The comfortable chairs and tufted cushions were inviting but alarmingly positioned directly below huge, globe chandeliers, hanging from ecru-painted ceilings, all gilt laden and glowing. "Mother Mary," Dehlia worriedly prayed under her breath, "I hope the chandeliers don't break off and fall upon us all! May Christ and His Saints stand between us and harm!"

She looked around and observed large, sparkling clean windows enclosing her with light. Each of them had beautiful stained glass transoms above them, glittering in warm colors of ruby red and golden amber. The furniture was lavishly upholstered in cut velour and decorated with wood. There was even a "fainting couch" in the ladies parlor for theatrical women to swoon and fall upon! Dehlia was relieved to find that her previously dismal steerage passage to America was a thing of the past. Luckily for her, she thought, it was not to be repeated this time!

Instead of going to her stateroom, where there were no windows, Dehlia preferred to walk about on the outdoor deck and watch the changing landscape go by. She had been told by the conductor that the steamboat would be traveling at the fast clip of eight miles per hour. She would have to be vigilant and attentive to view it all in just the short weeks' time she had until they arrived at the St. Louis levee. As she strolled along the deck of *The City of St. Louis*, she overheard a few passengers discussing the treacherous falls of the Ohio River.

"Oh yes Sir!" one astute gentleman announced to one of his comrades. "I understand the falls near the river town of Louisville, Kentucky are actually a series of rapids where this mighty river drops off."

"That fact actually makes me a bit nervous, my friend!" a man standing with him answered back.

Dehlia was curious to learn how the steamboat would navigate them to safety. Glancing around her, she noticed the passengers on *The City of St. Louis* steamboat were of various nationalities and races. There were German, Polish, English, French, and even Irish like the kindly officer that took her ticket. She strolled by another group of passengers, all animatedly gesturing with their hands while talking amongst themselves, when she heard a man loudly exclaim, "Why Gustave, don't you know that New Orleans is the second busiest port in the United States now?" Knowingly he continued, "6,000 bales of cotton and 4,000 sacks of cottonseed can be unloaded and reloaded in as few as eleven hours!"[36]

"Amazing!" thought Dehlia. Her brothers would be impressed with the diligence and magnitude of the workers here in America. I must write home and let them all know of the progress this great land is making. Maybe I could

---

[36] *On the Water, Inland Waterways, 1820-1890., amhistory.si.edu/*

convince one of them to make the journey over as well? She mused as she paused beside the group to absorb all the information she had overheard.

"Sir?" Dehlia asked of a rather stout old man in the group. "Do you know of the dangers that lurk ahead of us on this voyage? Are we safe onboard this steamboat now?

The old man turned to her and replied, "Oh my young lady! Do you not know of the many steamers that have been run aground on our last leg of our transport? Why, don't you know the Missouri River is known by all the pilots of these boats as "the Misery- a river like no other!"[37]

"No, I have not heard Sir!"

"And, don't you know the Missouri River enters into the mighty Mississippi, the big old river we will be turning onto after we dock at Cairo, Illinois?"

Noticing Dehlias' frantic face and recognizing a willing victim to share his horror stories with, the old man proceeded to elaborate in detail.

"Oh aye Miss, my old friend George Catlin, an artist who has indeed traveled along these parts painting portraits of the Indians, told me the Missouri River is "too thick to drink, and too thin to plow. It is more like watery mud and the current does indeed run fast as the channel shifts. He described dead trees, called snags, sticking out of the water only to grab ahold of the boats like bony fingers and try to bring them down into a watery grave!"

"Oh Sir, that is a scary image to think upon!" Dehlia

---

[37] *georgetownsteamboats.com*

exclaimed.

"Indeed young lady, and I don't doubt old Catlin was speaking the truth. Why he traveled for a short time back in the '30's with the Missouri General William Clark, exploring the upper Missouri River and painting pictures of that vanishing race of people!" he proudly added.

"God dammit Earl!" another old man, handsome in his handlebar mustache, standing next to him added. "Pardon me Miss," he said aside to Dehlia, "but don't be getting this young lady all upset with your talk of doom and gloom! Don't you see you are upsetting her?" he said to the presumed friend of George Catlin.

"Well, you old codger! I suppose you don't remember the explosion of the Sultana back in '65, do ya?" he asked. "Those 1,800 Union veterans and passengers didn't know what was comin' when the three faulty boilers blew them sky high!"

Dehlia shivered with the thought that she might actually die before she located Annie.

"Don't you know that steamboat was on a regular run up the Ole' Mississippi, just like this one?" the old man smugly implied.

"Earl, I warned you!" the mustachioed man frowned, "Don't upset the girl so much."

"Oh that's alright Sir, I need to know of what might be ahead of me. You see, for too long I have gone merrily along in my life, not questioning my path nor conscious of the pitfalls I might encounter. I only desire to know the truth Sir!"

The second old man paused a few minutes to look at Dehlia and then replied, "Well, I suppose one has the right to know what might lie ahead of him but my old buddy here was just yanking your chain a bit, you might say!"

"What do you mean?"

"First of all, the Missouri River does combine with the Mississippi River but further up in the state of Missouri, a little further on past St. Louis where we end our journey. Sure, snags and dangerous roots do show up along the route we are going but these are modern times Miss and these old pilots are plenty experienced in avoiding the pitfalls, and, I can assure you the pilot of this boat has checked the boilers numerous times since we boarded. I can almost guarantee we will all be quite safe." He chuckled as he turned with a grin toward his old friend."

"Aye, but tell her more about those old pilots, my friend, and their superstitions." His stout friend interjected.

"Well, sure they all have their own ideas and reasons for being superstitious." The second man agreed. "For instance, you will notice there is never a stateroom marked with the number 13, a truly unlucky number that would put a "hoodoo", a curse on the boat. And, of course, the thirteenth letter of the alphabet is "M" so no one names their boat beginning with that letter."

"Yah, but what about the sunken boats *Maria* and the *Moselle*? Those are good examples of hoodoo!" the stout man added. "Yeah, and what about the pilots superstitions about color, heh? A white cat means trouble, rats bring good luck, never throw anything off the head of the boat because it is bad luck to pass over your own trash, AND never let the calliope play "Home Sweet Home!"

Just as he said that, the calliope on board *The City of St. Louis* busted out with that very tune! All three of them jumped in place from the fright!

"Oh my, you people here in America have more superstitions and sayings than my Irish clan at home!" Dehlia stammered. "Whatever is that loud kind of music? How do they create it, and where does it come from?"

The two old men sheepishly looked at Dehlia and began to apologize for upsetting her.

"We are so sorry for giving you a scare, Miss. We were just having a bit of fun to pass the day away. No more lies will be passing over our lips." The second old man added.

"I do know a little about that big ole' steam organ, called the calliope." He volunteered. "Some people call them a steam piano, as it plays alike with a keyboard. Sorry for forgetting my manners Miss, my name is Jack Swain and this here is Earl, my verbose cousin. We travel around the country and up and down these rivers promoting the most wonderful operonicon, the steam car of the muses!" he bragged.

"Pleased to know ye, I think?" Dehlia giggled back. "How does this contraption work, Sir?"

"Why, it's a musical instrument, Miss, a wondrous invention that produces sound by sending steam through rather large whistles, much like the whistles on a locomotive. Most of the calliopes have a player up on deck, happily belting out their favorite tunes, but if you listen long enough, you will notice some off-pitch notes in the tune. Each note is largely affected by the temperature of the steam. Occasionally we hold our hands up to cover our ears from the glaring sound, but we are working on that, aren't we Earl?" he laughed.

"Yes, to be sure, but now we need to move on Miss. Hope we didn't scare you too much with our loose talk of danger, now. Best of luck to you in your journey. God speed."

"*Slan go foil.*" Dehlia waved as they turned to go. Well, she thought to herself, there are jokesters all around and those two certainly have the gift of gab. I'm just glad those two old men decided to fess up and tell the truth. Honey may be sweet but no one licks it off a briar! I think I'm going to practice keeping my thoughts to myself instead of having them written all over my face for others to make fun of!

On the second day of her trip, while perched upon a bench that was tacked down to the deck to prevent swaying, Dehlia caught a glimpse of a fellow travelers' newspaper with an illustration on the front showing a "bomb thrown by anarchist cutting down police and a drawing of a priest giving the last rites to a wounded officer in a nearby police station."[38]

---

[38] *History.1800s.about.com*, Robert McNamara, *The 1886 Haymarket Square Riot in Chicago*

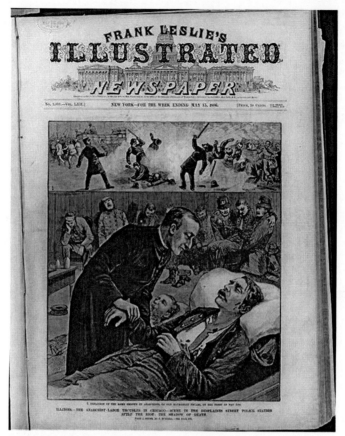

Illinois - The anarchist-labor troubles in Chicago from a
sketch by C. Bunnell

As she stared at the picture, the blood began to slowly
drain from her face. The gentlemen reading the newspaper
looked up and saw her staring at the letters emboldened
across the page.

"Ah yes, young lady, you have every right to be upset by
these headlines. As a business owner I can only curse the
union heathens that want to bring mayhem down on the
heads of their employers! We kindly give the starving masses
of unemployed jobs and they return the favor by striking for

higher wages and better working conditions! A pox of them all!" he spat out and threw the newspaper on the floor, angrily stepping on it as he walked away. The headline glared, "BOMB THROWN BY ANARCHISTS."

Dehlia gingerly picked up the tattered paper and began reading the text.

"On May 1, 1886, a large May Day parade was held in Chicago, and two days later, a protest outside the McCormick plant resulted in a person being killed. A mass meeting was called to take place on May 4, to protest what was seen as brutality by the police. The location for the meeting was peaceful, but the mood became confrontational when the police tried to disperse the crowd." The story went on, "As scuffles broke out, a powerful bomb was thrown. Witnesses later described the bomb, which was trailing smoke, sailing about the crowd in a high trajectory. The bomb landed and exploded, unleashing shrapnel. The police drew their weapons and fired into the panicking crowd. The policemen fired their revolvers for a full two minutes. Seven policemen were killed. Four civilians were also killed with more than 100 persons injured. The largest labor union in the United States, the Knights of Labor, is being blamed."

As the unsettling impact of the news began to flow over Dehlia, she thought only of the parallel image of Michael, seething with resentment after witnessing innocent children being shot. She shook her head to keep the horrible images at bay but the similarity of the turmoil began to overwhelm her. Imagine brutish landowners, and in this case, owners of the McCormick Harvesting Machine Company, locking out their workers and hiring strikebreakers! Scabs, her Da would have labeled them! Why can't people solve their problems peacefully like the good Lord intended? Isn't an eight-hour workday enough for the businessmen and their hypocritical boards to get their share of blood from a worker? Where is the compassion for each other? I pray my new country doesn't go through the repressions and reprisals like Ireland. While a person needs to stand up for their beliefs, I think they should be willing to compromise and listen to each other. I don't know, thought Dehlia despairingly, perhaps I am just weary of strife. At one time I would have fought against oppression. Now I just want to seek Annie and be wrapped in her arms of peace and contentment.

Dehlia was worn out from the excitement of the trip so she rested in the deck chairs as much as possible and tried to steer clear of men and their ravings. Arrgh, I do think broken Irish is better than clever English! She tried to keep her anxious mind on thoughts of more pleasant things. She remembered her Da's twinkling smile and would often pull out the photo of her Mam, all wrapped up and snug in her shawl. How she wished she could enjoy a conversation with her now. She mused over the games she and her brothers would sometimes play after chores were done and, she dreamed about Michaels' beautiful blue eyes. Dehlia counted her blessings for the many good people God had sent her way. There had been feisty Mary, sweet and shy Charles, the kind old lady in Castle Clinton and Clionna, a giggling breathe of fresh air! She gave thanks for Mrs. Vanderbilt and her support. Why, there are angels are all around us! Just like her Mam once told her, "If God sends you down a stony path, may He give you strong shoes!"

When the week of river travel was over, Dehlia gathered her luggage and gratefully stepped off the boat deck and onto the solid Missouri levee. She was surprised to see her sister and a rather tall man, both waving their arms frantically, trying to catch her attention. Dehlia gathered up all her belongings and ran with all her might into her sisters' arms!

"Annie! Oh Annie! How happy I am to be here!"

"Aye, *mo chuisle*, not as happy as I am that you are here!" Annie cried with wet tears coursing down her plump cheeks. "This is my husband Frank, who welcomes you as well."

"Your sister and I welcome you most heartily." Frank said as he vigorously pumped Dehlias' hand in greeting. "Most welcome indeed. We only have to travel a short distance by foot to our house. Unfortunately, most of the streets and roadbeds are macadam, that's a sort of mud mixture with an occasional dressing of crushed limestone on top. They are adequate enough when it is warm and fair but treacherous in foul weather." He nervously continued talking, "I work in the brick yards there, or rather, for the Winkle Terra Cotta Company." Dehlia could sense Frank needed to brag about his career, so she begged him to continue.

"I'm a craftsman, a skilled mold man. We make all the house trimmins for architects and their lavish buildings. The cornices we create have great potential and our business is getting bigger by the day!" he embellished.

"Ach, Frank, let Dehlia catch her breath, now! Enough about work, dear." Annie chided.

"Annie, why did Mrs. Vanderbilt's solicitor call the area you live in Dogtown? Does everyone have dogs and animals roaming there?" Dehlia asked.

"I can answer that one for you Dehlia." Frank interrupted. "Clay is mined in the area and when it was first developed, hardworking men were needed in great numbers to mine it from the earth. The unique red clay is made into bricks that are fired to withstand tremendous heat, of course a valuable asset, don't you think? Well, these miners were gone for most of the day and kept vicious dogs chained up outside of their shanties to discourage, should we say, robbers and thieves from taking what little belongings they had."

"Enough now, you are scaring our dear Dehlia!" Annie laughed. "Come on sweetheart, let's get you home and comfortable. Frank and I want you to stay with us as long as you wish, don't we Frank?"

"Oh, most certainly! Gazing fondly at Annie, he said, "I love my wife, my little Irish rose, and I want her to be happy living in an Irish neighborhood that wraps its' loving arms around her. If it makes her comfortable to have her family with her, too, then who am I to resist? Let's all go home!"

Dehlia was delighted to see the tangible love Frank had for her sister. What a blessing it must be to be loved so earnestly and unselfishly! It is wonderful to know Annie has found someone as devoted to her as our Mam and Da were. Surely, it was enough?

Chapter Thirteen

Settling In

The first week of city life in St. Louis, living with Annie and Frank, was a welcome blur of activity and getting familiar with the routine of her hosts. Frank would arise early, eat a hardy breakfast while Annie would pack him a lunch to carry to his job. The brickyard was just a short distance from their house and easily traversed even in the foulest weather. Annie, however, would have to ride a horse drawn streetcar to reach her employment as a helper in the progressive kindergarten run by Miss Blow at Des Peres School.

"Arrah Dehlia!" Annie cried out as she was scurrying out the door. "I heard new cable powered streetcars will soon be coming to our town! I can't wait for them to slice more minutes off my commute to school! Goodness knows how shy I am of the horses' hooves since a pair of them almost cut my life short!"

That evening, when Annie, Frank and Dehlia were relaxing in the parlor, Dehlia asked Annie to tell her about her work in the schools.

"I don't understand this word "Kindergarten" Annie. It is German, I think. I know you work every day with young children but how do you teach them with the objects you had mentioned in your last letter to me? Do you play all day? Why in Ireland, don't you remember how the nuns used to crack the rulers over our fingers if we were not paying attention? Surely you do not do that Annie, for you are too kind!"

"Faith, Dehlia!" Of course I am kind! Annie laughed. "Yes, the term kindergarten is German for child, a sort of child's garden, so to speak. Let me tell you a little about our program and its' founder, Miss Blow." Annie excitedly began to explain. "She was born in St. Louis and actually grew up in the same area, Carondelet, as the school I teach in. In fact, our school, Des Peres, was the first school to offer public kindergarten, thanks to the superintendent of schools, Mr. William Torrey Harris. He was a wise man indeed! You see, Mr. Harris was successfully persuaded by Elizabeth Peabody, a pioneer in American kindergarten[39] to include kindergarten in the public schools. Miss Peabody advocated that education of children needed to be more than just learning the basics of reading and mathematics and to represent them with the pencil. They needed to also learn strong discipline and be proficient in the basic skills. Basic skills such as the training of hand and eye, developing the habits of cleanliness, politeness, self-control and industry."[40]

"When did this basic skill training begin to go into effect, Annie?"

"Oh, long before I came to America, dear one! I believe about 1871 or so.

---

[39] Cantor, Patricia, May 2013, Elizabeth Peabody, *America's Kindergarten Pioneer*, page 93, *naeyc.org/yc*
[40] *en.wikipedia.org/Elizabeth_Peabody*

After all Dehlia, the youth in America were being encouraged not to work for low wages in the factories. Reformers were taking a stand to end the abomination of child labor. My teacher, Susan Blow, became Miss Peabody's first student in the United States."

"Yes, and what about all the children coming to America with their immigrant parents?" Dehlia queried. "What did all the parents do with their children when they had to work? Remember, in Ireland, our Mam and Nana stayed home to care for us but over here there seems to be little extended family."

"Aye, you are a smart girl to see that dilemma. That is exactly why Miss Blow decided Kindergarten was so important to champion. Let me go back a little farther back to explain this phenomena, *Mo chuise!* Miss Blows' father, Henry Blow, built a beautiful limestone home in Carondelet along many other German families."

"Ah yes Dehlia," Frank interjected, "Germans tend to stick together just like any other group of people, or at least until the beer runs out!" he laughed.

Annie smiled and waited patiently for Frank to finish his analogy, then she began again. "He spoiled his little Susan but in a good way, with patience and education. Oh, she was a sharp little one, I understand! He sent her to some of the best schools and even to Germany to study but her education was cut short when the Civil War started in the United States."

"I understand America was split apart, opposing sides even within families." Dehlia stated.

"Ah yes Dehlia," Frank interrupted again. "But us

Germans were and are, pro-Union and against all who favor treating others as property."

"That's right Dear, and so when Miss Blow came back to St. Louis she began to formulate a plan to establish Kindergarten in St. Louis. In Germany, just like Miss Peabody, she had studied Friedrich Froebel's methods of educating our very youngest children, through loving discipline, hands- on interactive play as well as language, math and science. With so many children coming into school from diverse backgrounds, we needed to prepare them for school in a cohesive way."

"When you met Miss Blow in the hospital did you know this was the work you were meant to do?" asked Dehlia.

"No, not at first. Miss Blow was gravely ill and it took a while before she had the strength to inform me of her life's work, and of course, I wasn't feeling too well either. A strike in the head from a horse's hooves does not actually knock sense into one!" Annie gaily laughed.

"No, it took some time before we became friends but I admire her so much and of course, you know how I love children, even though Frank and I don't have any of our own. But you see, Miss Blow eventually trained me after we both recovered, and so I teach young, growing minds, in a wonderfully bright and cheerful room, full of low tables and short benches. Just the right size for little, wiggly bodies! We teach with objects that can be handled within small hands and the children are encouraged to explore with their minds. I love it so; I can't wait to go to begin every day!"

"Aye, she does love it!" Frank interjected.

"What do you mean, objects that can be handled with small hands, Annie?" Dehlia inquired. "Do the children learn crocheting and such?"

"No, no, they manipulate and fold small, jointed slates or flat rods to form letters and such." Seeing Dehlia's confusion, Annie continued. "Our slates are similar to the Gonigraph. The idea is that one can teach math to young children with flat rods connected by pivots. These pivots allow the flat rod to be twisted around to form all sort of possible geometrical figures. Now we understand that these can be used to create fancy figures and a few letters as well. Oh the children love using them!"

"Miss Blow and those of us lucky to be trained by her are thoroughly faithful to the idea, methods and means so carefully worked out and tested by Froebel in his 50 years of experience. Of course, the only modification they have made in St. Louis is that the making of the time of entrance five years old instead of three or four years of age. However, Miss Peabody stated once that gradually, it will be seen, that even at five, children have something to unlearn."[41]

---

[41] *Kindergarten Messenger, Nos. 1,2*, Jan., Feb., 1877 Vol. I, Cambridge, published by Elizabeth P. Peabody, pg. 4

Plaiting Material. Fifty Slats (a set), 10 inches long, for interlacing, to form geometrical and fancy figures.

No. 7. Plaiting (Interlacing Slats.)

SIXTEENTH GIFT.

Jointed Slats. A Set of Jointed Slats with 3, 6, 8 and 16 links. Four jointed pieces a set.

shs.umsystem.edu

"I envy your feeling of accomplishment Annie. I think I need to be looking for gainful employment and stop being such a burden to you and Frank." Dehlia pondered as she watched Annie cheerfully cutting up colored paper into 10" slats, ready for the next days' lessons in math.

"Now darling, don't worry about looking for a job yet," she admonished Dehlia. "The next thing we need to do is get you a pretty new dress and fix your hair in an upswept style. Miss Blow said we must look professional at all times!

Goodness knows, you have grown up so quickly little sister, and you are in desperate need of a new set of clothes befitting your age! Until then, continue to stitch your beautiful lace collars and cuffs. They are such incredible works of art! Build up your inventory of gorgeous laces so we can show them around to the seamstresses in town. When we have time we will see what we can do to find employment for you! I want you to enjoy your stay in our home, *Mo Chuisle*. Mam and Da too, would want you to feel safe and sound with us for a while Dehlia. In due time you can seek employment, in due time."

"Aye Annie, but you know what Da always said, "A thank you does not pay the fiddler!""

"Oh my darling, fiddle around on your lace for now!" Annie laughed. "Praise God, I am so glad you are here with us."

Dehlia thoughtfully picked up her lace bobbin and began crocheting the intricate collar she had been working on, all the while mulling in her mind the numerous changes that had been wrought in only three years. In that short length of time she had evolved from an idealistic youth to an unraveling, despairing maiden. She had single-handedly braved the rigors of a wide ocean, worked for gainful employment to become an efficient young lady and now, even though safely harbored in her sisters' home and crushed to her ample bosom, she must transform herself once again. It is so hard to start anew each time the road of my life takes a twisty turn, Dehlia thought. Oh well, *bi'onn gach tosach lag*, every beginning is weak! Our Mam used to say this when things got tough and she and Da had to start over raising a flock of sheep or when the crops failed to meet their expectations. *Bi'onn gach tosach lag!*

Dehlias' new beginning was a sporadic patchwork of daily stitching on her lace projects in Annie and Franks' home and wearily lighting candles at St. Patricks' Church on Sixth and Biddle streets. The large Catholic Church was located in the "Patch", a distinct neighborhood of small clapboard houses where several families often lived together within one dwelling. St. Louis was a population of 43% Irish, mostly immigrants, who brought their grudges and political gang mentality with them to the new world. The so-called "Kerry Patch" consisted of violent men whose chief amusement consisted of "pummeling out each other's eyes."[42] As Dehlia traipsed the streets and wound her way back and forth, as a shuttle on a loom forms the warp and welf in fabric, she discerned a rippling undercurrent of cross-cultural hatred.

"Annie, I didn't leave Ireland to be confronted by senseless violence in the streets! I know wrongs need to be righted but why do men believe they have to band together to bully those who don't perceive political issues to be the same as their opinions?" Dehlia vehemently exclaimed one night after dinner.

"Well, listen to this *Liebling!*" Frank interrupted Dehlia, as he glanced at Annie for approval before he spoke. "It has long been difficult to live in St. Louis. You see, there was a terrible flood here in 1849 and after that followed a cholera epidemic.

---

[42] *St.LouisIrishHistory-KerryPatch*

To top that off, then came what the newspapers called The Great Fire, which destroyed most of the city. It has been established about 10 percent of the population died from the combination of these three disasters!" Frank continued on. "Now about this time, the German and Irish immigrants were beginning to enter the city and luckily for them, at a time that was particularly convenient for rebuilding! However, the Germans were given the skilled jobs like mine and the poor Irish were given manual, unskilled and unwanted as well as dangerous jobs. The burly Irish were scrappers you see, and fought often with others, as well as among themselves, for the right to work. However, in my opinion, the immigrant Germans and Irish were the two groups who salvaged St. Louis and built it from the ground up. My own Papa was one of the men who helped to save the city from almost total destruction, I am proud to say!" Frank proudly said.

"I heard some residents say that is why all the rebuilt homes had to be constructed from brick as opposed to wooden frame." Annie stated.

"Yes, Liebling, it is and these new brick homes can be considered to be built on the backs of the stout Irish, who did all the grunt work. Did you know that after the Great Fire, at least twenty seven clay mines were opened to create brick, the much needed commodity?"

"Aye Darling," Annie answered. "Now tell Dehlia about the Irish hero, Phelim O'Toole, who was a hero the night of the tragic Southern Hotel fire." She asked.

"Ach, you are right indeed! Frank agreed. Old Phelim O'Toole was born in Dublin, Ireland about 1848 and immigrated to St. Louis in 1866 or so, landing himself smack dab in the Kerry Patch! He became a firefighter but lost his life when he was only thirty-two years of age."

"What happened?" Dehlia inquired.

"The massive Southern Hotel was located down at Fourth and Elm Streets and was a six story luxury hotel, with all the trappings a rich person would want while boarding there. When O'Toole got there he saved many patrons and was considered quite the hero. The story goes that O'Toole responded to another small fire, the night of July 6, 1880, on Locust Street. I was told the fire extinguisher he was using exploded on this chest. He cried out, "I am killed!" and they buried him in Calvary Cemetery, as befitting a brave warrior."

Phelim O'Toole - stlfire4.loudclick.net/home.aspx

"Well, I for one am proud of someone from our homeland who valiantly saved others rather than becoming a brute!" Annie righteously stated. "I think men like O'Toole and the values they represent only help, rather than hinder, what we

Irish are truly about!"

Frank looked up from the newspaper he was reading and said amazed, "Listen to this story if you have a mind to! It's another tale about the Old Southern Hotel. It seems that the authorities have just recently jailed a Mr. Hugh Brooks, an attorney no less, who was implicated in the 1855 murder of a certain Charles Preller. This Mr. Brooks is appealing to the Supreme Court for a new trial, says here that Brooks stated, "He never intended to kill him!"

"Wait a minute." Annie spoke. "Wasn't he the one who left his traveling salesman friend Preller, at the hotel, where they found his body in a large trunk with a note attached?"

"Aye, hear what the police say about that!" Frank began to read the paper out loud again. "The body of Preller was found in one of the trunks with a note attached reading: "So perish all traitors to the great cause." "Ahem," Frank continued, "it appears Brooks was trying to pin the murder on the Fenian Brotherhood. That squirrel Brooks was finally caught in Australia and returned to America to stand trial for the cold bloodied murder. Let's see, I murdered someone but I really didn't mean it, it just happened and it's not my fault! I hope they hang him!"

A chill went down Dehlia's spine. Even here in America the fingers of the Devil were caught up in the puckered threads of malcontent. The knots in her stomach tightened with the dreaded feeling that doom and destruction had intently followed her over from Ireland. She felt the blood drain from her face.

Alarmed, Annie noticed her pallor and quickly said, "I

think it high time we buy a beautiful dress for you and have your curly hair trained to stay in place, sweet one! In fact, why don't we book an appointment to have your photo taken as well, and send it home for Mam and Da to put on their mantel over the fireplace? How they would love to know I am taking good care of you and that we are all prospering! What do you think Frank? Should we do that?"

"Why of course my darling, whatever your heart desires!"

True to her word, Annie arranged for Dehlia to be fitted with a new dress and get her hair styled in a more mature fashion. She booked an appointment with A. J. Fox, a popular photographer on Fourth and Olive Streets, for eleven o'clock on October 1, 1866. The wheels were set in motion to transform Dehlia from a disconsolate emigrant into a fortuitous young lady. However, Dehlia knew it would take more than pretty dresses and baubles to transform her back into the happy girl she had been before she left Ireland, before Michaels' death and before her spirit was robbed of all its' joy.

The day of the appointment began as all the previous days had since arriving in St. Louis. Frank arose early and jauntily walked to work, happy that he could work at such a fabulous place as the Winkle brickyard. Annie rushed to catch the streetcar, which Dehlia continued to call the "tram" as they preferred to call it in New York City. As portly Annie ran out the door, she glanced back and yelled above the street noises, "Smile pretty, *Mo Chuisle*, you never know what God has in store for you!"

Left to her own, Dehlia began to gather up the bag that contained her brand new dress and shoes. She was in a hurry to walk to the beautician who was going to trim her bangs and style her long curly hair. Then she would have to scramble into her new dress and arrive at the photographers' studio by 10:45 prompt! Despite her own reservations, Dehlia was anxious and excited to be able to transform herself into a lady! *Mai'ther* always stressed a person should strive to be more proud of the inside of their soul rather than the vanity of the surface but, oh how wonderful it will feel to put my best foot forward! Dehlia thought. Here, in this smallish, but significant town, no one suspects my traitorous past. They don't know what a coward I was, hiding behind my parents' terror, how utterly simplistic I thought the World was! No one questions me about my past subversive actions and the hideous consequences that occurred because of them. Just like Matthew 5 in the Bible declares, "it rains on the just as well as the unjust." The Priest said, "Don't envy those who do evil or lie but quietly go about your Father's business." Perhaps this mask of pretty clothing will hide the raw edges of my inner seams and allow me to begin my life anew. Does the good Lord know how frayed and fragile I feel right now? Oh Michael, why did you leave me to hold onto this burden all by myself? Why were you allowed to die and me to survive? I will never understand the Lords' ways and why he brought me to this new land, wretch that I am!

While Dehlia was musing on these self-deprecating thoughts, she watched as the hair dresser skillfully swept her long reddish-brown hair high up on her head and pulled it into a very neat and tidy bun. With her capable fingers, she poked and prodded Dehlias' wispy bangs into springy little curls that daintily hugged her face.

"Those adorable little "Josephine Curls" make your eyes shine and I believe, a pert bow at the back of your hair bun would be just the ticket to finish the look!" the lady exclaimed. "I have just the one to match the color of your mauve dress." Dehlia was pleased when she glanced in the mirror with her new garment and shoes on. Her new hairstyle made her appear more mature and the dress, ah! The dress was a beautiful shade of mauve. The lightweight silk material was stamped with a watery, wavelike effect the French call "moiré". It had a little lace ruffled stand up "officers' collar" layered with delicate embroidery work of tiny beads, all spilling down over the slightly puffy shoulders of the dress and cascading down the bodice. The bodice had what the fashion magazines called a "princess line" with a series of pin tucked panels racing rigidly down the low front to the fairly cascading skirt. The flowing skirt was draped over a small crinoline in the rear and stopped just short of her ankles. She pulled on the short white ladies' gloves her sister Annie had loaned her, tugging and stretching the soft fabric over her needle pricked fingers and buttoning each wrist with a tiny pink pearl button.

"Oh my, you do look beautiful, my dear!" The kind hairdresser remarked. "The dusky hue goes well with your complexion and hazel eyes." Dehlia did feel remarkably beautiful as well. "Let's see if your little doll hat will happily perch on the front of your head!" the hairdresser added.

Dehlia attached her hat to the crown of her head, while the hairdresser carefully turned one half of the brim up into a jaunty salute! "There now, perfect! I do think your hat becomes you better than some of those tall, flowerpot hats the ladies are all wearing now!"

"I know mam, but to tell you the truth, I would much rather be wearing a simple straw hat or even a bonnet. I really don't want to draw much attention to myself."

"Well, dear, you are a natural beauty and you should be proud of it. Go conquer the world!"

Thanking her hairdresser for the kind attention, Dehlia left her house with a smile and giddy with the anticipation of having a photo taken to send back to her folks in Ireland. Wouldn't they be amazed by her transformation? She gleefully thought.

Now if she could only get down the street in one piece and not disheveled, in adequate time for her appointment. As she ventured out to the sidewalk on Olive Street, the crowds of people began to ebb and swell. The bodies of pedestrians flowed like water over and around her. She felt like a small pebble in a brook that tries valiantly to hold the course only to find itself dislodged and floating along with the current. At last she arrived at the address of the renowned photographer, a Mr. A. J. Fox. Dehlia was a little bewildered from the crush of the crowds by the time she pushed open the entrance door. She staggered into the portico and opened the impressive glass door of the photography studio. She glanced around the parlor area and noticed that this was indeed, a grand place. She immediately felt a pang of regret for letting Annie urge her to have her picture taken. Embarrassed and feeling totally out of place, she looked up and saw a friendly pair of blue eyes appraising her. They were languidly taking her in, from head to toe. She noticed the face the eyes belonged to also included a nice smile.

The face said, "Are you our eleven o'clock appointment?"

"I believe so, Sir." The face, and the eyes, and the nice smile beamed back at her.

"You know," the voice gently remarked, "you are a lovely young lady but I think I have just what you need to make your portrait complete. Let's see, where is it?" He looked under the counter and pulled out a fabric corsage of a white tea rose, daintily attached to a lace handkerchief. "Ah ha! Just the ticket! Pin this little beauty onto your right shoulder. It will compliment your beautiful complexion and your perfect rosebud lips." Not sure if the young man was admiring her person or brazenly teasing, Dehlia accepted the corsage and nervously attached the flowers to the shoulder of her dress. Task completed, he politely asked her to sit down and wait while he went to tell Mr. Fox his next sitting had arrived. After a short time Mr. Fox, the photographer, introduced himself and began talking about his passion for his art. He put Dehlia completely at ease and after a few minutes of fidgeting with his camera equipment, he snapped several images of her sitting in an ornate wooden chair as well as standing beside a bureau with a veined marble top. She was sure the furniture in his studio was expensive for it was made entirely of deep cherry and inlaid with strings of pale linden wood. She had dusted many tables just like it at the Vanderbilts' in New York. Dehlia removed her gloves in order to feel the soft grain of the wood and tentatively trace her fingers over the veins in the cold marble top. After the photo session wrapped up, Mr. Fox instructed Dehlia to return in a week and pick up and approve her pictures.

"Well, I hope I can walk back home without being accosted in the streets by that massive throng of people!" Dehlia casually remarked to Mr. Fox before she turned to leave.

"You must have felt like a fish swimming upstream!" Mr. Fox laughed. "Why, don't you know President Cleveland is in town today? His pretty new wife Francis and his whole political entourage rode the "Presidential Special," into town. A Pullman Special for sure! The whole lot of them are in St. Louis for a few days on his "Goodwill tour" of the western States, whipping up support and monetary gains as well! I suppose the crowds you encountered along the way were rushing to see the train pull in. Why all the newspapers were touting it to be a glorious site to see! The festivities should be winding down now so rest assured, you will surely have an easier time getting back home."

"A Pullman Special?" Dehlia asked. "I know about trains, Sir, but I don't understand what a Pullman is?"

"Indeed, young lady! A Pullman Special is what we call the luxury rail car a Mr. George Mortimer Pullman, himself born into a poor family of carpenters, has built and bartered. He made himself a glorious fortune by leasing these lavish cars to the rail companies. Goodness knows," he continued, "I'm sure our good President and his lovely wife are riding in high-style, sitting atop lavish, green velvet cushions and being waited upon by an attendant dedicated to meeting all their needs. Why, I suppose their attendant is even raising and lowering the dark green shades for them as they wish!" Smiling at the thought of such elegant excess, Mr. Fox winked at Dehlia, proud he could establish himself as a knowledgeable man.

Smiling back at the verbose Mr. Fox, Dehlia thanked him again for his time and expertise. As she was leaving, she remembered borrowing the fabric flower, turned around and unpinned the white rose corsage from her gown.

"Why, I almost forgot to return this!" She nervously placed it on the counter, glanced up and thanked the handsome young man who had suggested attaching it to her dress in the first place.

"The pleasure is all mine, Miss." The blue eyes sparkled as the deep voice said, "And please, my name is George." Flustered and just a tiny bit embarrassed by the singular attention he was devoting to her, Dehlia tried as gracefully as she could to exit the studio door. She felt herself flush warm and her face blush as she ran down the stoop to retrace her steps back home to Annie and Franks' house. It wasn't until she was several blocks down the street, when to her dismay she realized she had dropped Annie's precious white gloves somewhere along the way! Annie will be so upset! I've lost them! She thought. Annie and Frank have a few extra comforts and extravagances now they are both working at good jobs but what a dimwit I am for losing an article of clothing Annie had scrimped and saved for. It's all on account of the flirting that young man, that George! It's been a long time since I allowed anyone to turn my head and see what happened? She admonished herself. What a terrible, disappointing end to a day that held so much promise!

Chapter Fourteen

The Future or the Past?

Dehlia fretted the rest of the afternoon over losing Annie's gloves. She tried to labor on her crocheting but had to eventually rip out most of the stitches for lack of concentration. She put down her lace collars and began crocheting a small purse out of coarse cotton threads but her mind circled around and around, just like the pattern on her latest endeavor. When Annie finally arrived home, Dehlia explained how badly she felt for dropping the gloves on the street and losing them.

"It was his gawking that made me forget what I was doing Annie!" she said, blaming the young man.

"Oh Dehlia, I must admit I did love those gloves but don't trouble yourself with regret because they mostly languished in my bureau drawer! Remember, you helped me pack my kit in Ireland all those long years ago and I didn't have but a few pitiful rags to stuff in it! In time I will buy myself some new gloves. Until then it is much more important that I have, at last, my baby sister's lovely face to gaze upon!"

Just when Dehlia was going to remark to her sister that Annie had been far better off before Dehlia had stepped off the boat in St. Louis, they heard three firm knocks against the wooden door of Annie and Franks' home. Dehlia thought better of reminding Annie, yet again, what a burden she was and turned instead to see who was so insistent to talk to them. When she opened the front door she saw the gentle face of George, the photographers' assistant, holding out a narrow box to her and wearing a tentative smile. In the other hand he was clutching a bouquet of dainty white rosebuds.

"Pardon me, Miss, but you dropped these gloves as you stumbled, er, rushed out the door earlier today. I thought you would miss them and wanted to return them to you as soon as I got off work. And, because you looked so pretty with a white rose at your cheek, I brought you some tiny rosebuds, just opening now." He randomly continued, a little unnerved to be standing right in front of Dehlia, toe to toe!

"Why thank you, Mr., um?"

"George Watts, at your service and you are Miss Fleming?" He inquired.

"Please come in Mr. Watts," Annie begged. "I'm Dehlias' sister. I believe my baby sister has quite forgotten her manners! Come in and have a cuppa for your kindness."

"Thank you but I can't stay. I have a night class meeting in thirty minutes at the School and Museum of Fine Arts. It is imperative I attend tonight in order to pass my first year exams." George said emphatically, "But I would like to obtain your permission to ask Miss Dehlia out. I have been fortunate enough to garner tickets to see the St. Louis Brown Stockings. I was wondering if she would like to go to a baseball game?" He turned around, suddenly remembering the object of his attention, winked and asked, "Would you care to accompany me, Dehlia?"

Dehlia just stared, not knowing what to say. She was grateful for the returned gloves but not sure she trusted her fragile feelings for this tall, young man.

"Of course Dehlia will go with you!" Annie interjected into the dreadful silence looming over them. "She will be pleased to."

"Wonderful! I will be by to pick you up Sunday afternoon at one." George replied with a nervous smile and with a nod to Dehlia, he stepped back out into the evening.

When the door was safely shut, Dehlia found her voice. "I am most certainly NOT going out with that man! I haven't had so much as a conversation with him and I don't know him from Adam!"

"But Dehlia, all that Victorian formality is old-fashioned in America today! Young women, like you, need to meet nice young men and go out courting. You haven't looked at another boy since losing your Michael in Ireland. Don't you think your heart has mended well enough to give romance a try once again?"

"No I don't," Dehlia retorted. "I will never love another man like I did Michael! Don't you see I am broken! I will never let my heart be fooled again, and anyway, that George has an English last name! I hate the English! Those people made our family starve and shed Michaels' blood! Two Englishmen tried to take advantage of me on the ship over and an ole' English biddy made my life miserable in New York City! I will not give him the time of day, thank you very much. Not now, not ever!"

Annie just sighed, hoping Dehlia would change her mind a few days from now. After all, the pig in the sty doesn't know the pig going along the road, she thought to herself. My baby sister doesn't realize how pleasant it is to journey along the winding ribbon road of Life with another person who cares for you. Why, my Frank is from Germany, where the cruel Kaiser reigns, but my husband is a constant source of happiness to me. If I had let my narrow-mindedness hem in my heart, I would not know the contentment I feel now. Perhaps Dehlia just needs a bit of time to heal the wounds in her soul. Why, it's easy to halve the potato where there's love, I know!

Instead, Annie merely remarked, "Don't pigeonhole everyone you meet, Dehlia. Here in America we are all immigrants, coming from somewhere. We need to learn to get along and work together, be they English or not!"

Undeterred by Annie's prompting, Dehlia gathered up the fresh bouquet, rushed to the back door in the kitchen and threw the white roses in the dustbin. Turning around and dusting off her hands, she declared, "There, Mr. George What's -Your -Name, that is where your flower message belongs! Why of all the nerve, giving me roses, the flower symbol of love before you even know me! What an *eejet!*"

Much to Dehlia's dismay, Sunday afternoon arrived too soon for her liking. Annie was patient, as well as persistent and Dehlia reluctantly agreed to go out one time with the Englishman since he had been gallant enough to return Annie's gloves. She owed him that much, she unwillingly agreed. She mechanically got ready for her date with George

Watts but intertwined with her vulnerable feelings for Michael were surprising thoughts of this tender new man in her life. She heard a knock at the door, shook off her exposed emotions and rushed downstairs, anxious, once again, to get the ordeal over with. When she opened the door she glanced up into the sky and stared again into the kindly eyes of the young man. Without having said a word to her, Dehlia would have had to be blind to see that his eyes revealed feelings of immutable acceptance and admiration for her. What possessed this man to be able to see through to her very soul? What did he glimpse as he looked so carefully? Did he see a fugitive with sins of the past? A stupid, sleazy girl to be taken advantage of? Or a grown woman who has steeled her heart against feeble promises? Taken aback and stiffly unyielding, Dehlia thought to herself, nothing good can come of this!

"Hello." George began, a little nervously. "You are looking quite lovely today, Miss Dehlia. I brought you a small posy of acacia and pansies." Grinning, he said, "I am sure you know they are the fragrant symbols of friendship. These," he gallantly presented, "I cheerfully offer up to you."

"Why, thank you, um, George. I guess I'm ready to go." Dehlia delicately took a whiff of the small bundle of flowers. She picked up her parasol from the large ginger jar at the door and gingerly took ahold of his proffered arm. Duly shaded from the sun by the umbrella, the two of them began a nervous walk to Sportsman's Park. While they were strolling along, George began to explain the game of baseball and the history behind the favorite local St. Louis team called the Brown Stockings, much later to be called The Browns and decades more, The Cardinals.

Sportsman's Park, with the diamond located on the northwest corner, circa 1902. Chicago Daily News - The Library of Congress-American Memory SDN-005703, Chicago Daily News negatives collection, Chicago History Museum.

"When I was growing up here in St. Louis, Sportsman's Park was originally called the Grand Avenue Ball Grounds."

"Wait," Dehlia stammered. "I thought you were from England."

"No, I was born and raised right here in good ole' St. Louie, but my Mother and Father both emigrated from Southern England when they were quite young. In fact, my father, Jeremiah, had quite an adventure aboard a whaling vessel when he was only eighteen! They are now naturalized citizens of the United States, and quite proud of it!" George added.

"Oh, I see. I had thought you to be newly arrived here, such as me." Dehlia remarked as she hesitated to glance up at tall George. Together, they entered the ballpark at the entrance to the grandstand on Grand Avenue. The main entrance was covered and located next to the park's office. As George and Dehlia stepped into the entrance enclosure she quickly counted four winding stairways in which the patrons could reach the grandstand. George continued to explain.

"No, we are proud to be called Americans, a melting-pot so to speak, of all heritages, races and religions." George cheerfully added. "Wait until you see this game, Dehlia, it is amazing! Why, the manager of the team, Charlie Cominsky has taken the St. Louis Browns through a winning fifth season in the American Association. The Browns have a good chance to win a second pennant in a row this year! So far, their stats are ninety-two and forty-six!" he proudly stated. "Perhaps they will win this game and seal the deal! You might just have brought them good luck, as you have me, my fair Dehlia!"

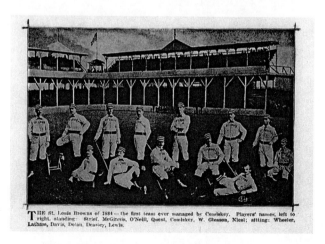

THE St. Louis Browns of 1884 — the first team ever managed by Comiskey. Players' names, left to right, standing: Strief, McGinnis, O'Neill, Quest, Comiskey, W. Gleason, Nicol; sitting: Wheeler, Latham, Davis, Dolan, Deasley, Lewis.

Dehlia glanced again at the animated, friendly face. Perhaps she had been too hasty to judge him. She began to relax and melt into the fever Americans call baseball.

"See those three private boxes near the roof, Dehlia? They are used by the officials and the press. They watch and report on the game from up there."

Casually looking around her, Dehlia noticed a powder room for the ladies to use at the back of the grandstand where they were sitting and a beer garden for the men beneath it. *Goodness*, she thought, *this baseball park is better appointed than the ship she had sailed in from Ireland!*

"Are you hungry Dehlia? Would you like to try a local food item to eat? I guarantee it is delicious!"

"Well, sure George, I suppose so. Do we have to go somewhere to buy one?"

"No" he handsomely smirked. "Wait and see. A concessionaire will be coming around in a little while to pass out piping hot sausages, each wrapped up in a bun of bread. He can hand us a couple then."

"Oh my, I have never seen such a thing!" Dehlia laughed. "How did they ever think of something like that?"

"Well, from what I have heard, our concessionaire, a Mr. Feuchtwanger, used to peddle these delicious sausages to the crowds here at the stadium but they were too hot to handle so in order to keep the customers from burning their hands, he offered his gloves as he passed the sausage down the row. Unfortunately," George laughed, "the customers often walked off with his gloves rather than returning them! Of course, this was a very unprofitable situation for old Feuchtwanger so his thrifty wife came up with the solution of long, soft rolls that fit the length of the sausage perfectly! They call these, "red hots! You will love them." He confidently pronounced.

Sure enough, the "red hots" were delicious and George and Dehlia giggled together when small bags of roasted peanuts were tossed to them as well. Dehlia had to laugh when her gallant escort would miss a bag, only to have it fall on the people in front of them. Embarrassed, George would explain he was not very good at everything "life threw at him". A few minutes later a powerful gust of wind rose up from beneath the stands and blew his straw boater off his head! George scrambled down to the dusty walkway and retrieved it, laughing and joking that even the wind wanted to play ball with him! She liked his humble nature and soon was completely at ease in his presence. Oh, it was a wonderful game! The pennant was sealed by the Brown Stockings and the crowds roared their approval.

After the game, Dehlia and George sauntered back to Annie's house a bit slower than the going.

"Why are you working as an assistant in a photographer's studio?" Dehlia questioned George when they were almost home.

"I only work there to earn enough money to pay my tuition at the Art School. I hope to become a portrait painter someday, and have my own studio to work in. Mr. Fox has been kind enough to hire me and let me work for him around my class schedule. I don't mind working at any job that will help to pay my bills. I'm not too proud to sweep the floors or take out the garbage." Dehlia began to look at George with renewed interest. *"Ah,"* she pondered as she slowly took in the length of the handsome man in front of her. *Da had a* saying, *"the true nature of someone's character is revealed through their eyes."*[43] *And aren't those beautiful eyes to be sure?* She thought to herself appraisingly.

Why, here is a man with similar values! She realized. Feeling comfortable with George by now, she cautiously started to talk and unravel the binding that contained her life. Piece by piece, she recounted the deeds that pricked at her heart and caused it to bleed. It felt good to finally release the pain and suffering she had experienced but had been cautioned to keep to herself. George was reverently silent as she told him about the terrible famine in Ireland and Michael's part in the revolution but not of her implication in the murder. Dehlia recognized that the Irishman's proverb, "one cannot be in a relationship with out accepting a person's friends, family and past affiliations." was definitely true. Would George think her foolish for her murderous indiscretion? She could not risk telling him now. Instead she continued to describe her horrific voyage across the ocean and how she was lucky enough to find work, albeit degrading, at the hotel, but which in turn, gave her the opportunity to work at the Vanderbilt's.

"When I worked at the Vanderbilt mansion a horrible woman poked fun of my name and called me a 'Bridgit', meaning an Irish girl of little worth. I don't understand why people feel the need to degrade others. Is it only to make them feel better about themselves?"

Without saying a word, George tenderly picked up her hand, gently placed his other one over it as if enclosing a

---

[43] *compassrose.org*

fragile rose. He looked deep into her eyes, as if searching her soul.

"We learned in our classical art class that Bridget is the Celtic goddess of fire and poetry. I choose to think of you as that. Don't let the spitefulness of others rule your thoughts." He bent his head down and kissed the top of her hand, as a gentleman would. George then backed up and asked, "Would you give me the pleasure of stepping out with me again next weekend? You are a most courageous and fascinating woman Dehlia. Your honesty has touched me to the core. I'm amazed that such a tiny slip of a girl could be so brave and hold so much passion within her heart. I am truly honored and humbled to know you."

Of course Dehlia gratefully accepted his friendship, for she would have been foolish not to, and over the course of the next three months, they became constant friends and companions.

Hand over arm, like an agreeable old married couple, they sauntered around the newly opened Botanical Gardens, chattering together about all of nature's beauty spread out around them. The Linnaean House was one of their delights to fully explore.

"This building is absolutely astonishing, George! I love to wander up and down the narrow isles inside."

"Yes indeed! The building is as amazing as the man it was named for, Carl Linnaeus."

"Who was he? Why did the Botanical Gardens name it after him? He didn't come from St. Louis, did he?"

"No, Carl Linnaeus was born in Sweden, long ago in 1707.

He was a scientist but is best known as a botanist. He was a teacher and had several students he called his "Apostles."

"What a strange term, apostles. That refers to the Bible, yes?"

"Well not exactly in his case." George laughed. "Linnaeus and his Apostles travelled around the world with expeditions funded by royal patronage, locating and identifying collections of flora and fauna. They also sailed on many voyages with trading companies and whalers."

"How do you know about all of this? Where do you get all your information?"

George smiled fondly, with a faraway look in his eye. "Ah, well my father, Jeremiah Watts was a whaler back in the day. He sailed for four years on the whaling vessel, The Ann Alexander, in 1845. He became very interested in drawing the leaves and landforms of the islands where he set port."

"Is that why you are so keen on art?"

"Ahhh, I suppose it is, clever girl! My father taught me to observe Nature closely. An artist creates on a two dimensional surface what he sees visually."

"Sort of like a magician, I think George!"

"Indeed, indeed! And I can observe you and I are both in need of some lemonade!"

Giggling, Dehlia placed her hand on George's arm and they hurried off to locate a lemonade stand to quench their parched throats.

Photocopy of October 1, 1903 photograph. Glass negative in Paul A. Kohl's office, Missouri Botanical Garden. VIEW FROM THE SOUTHEAST, SHOWING ORIGINAL CENTRAL CHIMNEY AND IRON ROOF RIDGE CRESTING - Missouri Botanical Garden, Linnaean House, 2345 Tower Grove Avenue, Saint Louis, Independent City, MO Photos from Survey HABS MO-1135-D

As the winter weather set in and their wonderland became icy, they laughed as they skated, arm in arm, on frozen ponds in Lafayette Park. They tightened their Henley skates with adjustable screws when they accidently slipped off their feet.

"Zounds, not again!" George cried when his skates pulled loose of his shoes, for the umpteenth time.

"Let's sit down on the bench awhile." Dehlia suggested. "Tell me a little about this beautiful park. When I asked Annie and Frank about it, they didn't seem to know much."

"Ahh, Lafayette Park is considered one of the first public parks in St. Louis and one of the oldest urban parks west of the Mississippi."

"The Mississippi River was the waterway I traveled up to St. Louis." Dehlia added.

"My father told me in 1868, five years before I was born

and my parents settled in St. Louis, a huge amount of money was raised through a municipal bond issue. With these funds, St. Louis was able to construct iron fences and benches around the park, like the one we are sitting on. They also had enough money to commission ad erect a bronze statue of Thomas Hart Benton."

"Who was this Mr. Benton? Did he lead a rebellion like our Irish Wolfe Tone?"

"Rebellion is not the word I would call the work he did. Benton was a lawyer and famous Senator from Missouri. I believe, if my memory serves me right, he came to St. Louis in about 1815 when the town was just a little muddy squalor of wood and stone buildings. He had two agendas, westward expansion and opposing the institution of slavery. He was a very flamboyant character."

"The town must have been very proud of his achievements because they wanted a statue to commemorate him."

"The sculptor was, interestingly enough, Harriet Goodhue Hosmer, a female."

"Oh my, I love that George! Just think, women can achieve great things in this day and age!"

"Actually, Miss Hosmer studied anatomy in private lessons at the St. Louis University medical school. I try to go to as many figure drawing classes as I can as well but while it is easy for me to attend, it was far more difficult for a woman to be allowed to participate."

"Amazing George! I am equally impressed with your knowledge about art and your city."

Blushing a bit, George replied, "I know it seems as if I am a fount of knowledge but it's just because I grew up here and have paid attention to St. Louis history. Anyway, thinking about the Hart statue has given me an idea."

"What idea? Are we going to another park to skate?"

"No, you just wait and see Dehlia! I have lots of tricks up my sleeve!"

One glorious day, George arrived at Annie and Franks' house in a rented buggy, pulled by a graceful dove gray horse. He nimbly jumped out of the drivers' seat, hitched the horse to the post and ran up the sidewalk to fetch Dehlia for another date. When she opened the door she gleefully exclaimed,

"Oh my George! How beautiful this horse and buggy is! Are we really going for a ride in this vehicle?" she asked.

"Yes we are! I rented this sleigh to whisk you over hill and dale in the snow today! Look how the sun glistens on the snow. It's a fairyland waiting to be experienced! Come on, climb up, it's a beautiful day to enjoy the sights of St. Louis! Here, let me wrap this wool blanket over your lap to keep you warm."

"Oh my George! This blanket is beautiful and warm, but so heavy!"

"Indeed it is! I borrowed it too! It's called a sleigh blanket, made of heavy horse hair so it will not blow off your lap during our carriage ride."

"You have thought of everything. Thank you for being so considerate of my comfort but won't you be cold too?"

"Nah, I have my comfortable corduroy trousers to keep

me toasty. I just want you to be warm and happy! Now, I know just the street to take you to. Let me be your valiant guide!" he teased. "You will be absolutely amazed at the wonderful homes tucked among the hillside there. Wait and see!"

As the merry couple raced and cruised over hill and dale, George stood up in the carriage, his arms spread askew and shouted out, "Afoot and light-hearted I take to the open road, healthy, free, the world before me. The long brown path before me leading wherever I choose!"

Chuckling along with her stalwart guide, Dehlia exclaimed, "Oh George! That is so fine! I didn't know you were such a grand poet!"

Laughing with delight, George said, "I am not a poet, fair lady of mine, but rather an "appreciator" of great literature! Walt Whitman, the man who penned these wise words, is the gentleman I aspire to be! Although I don't actually agree with the politics of this old man, I do admire his free verse. Noticing Dehlia's ardent attention, George continued his poetic rant. "Henceforth I ask not good-fortune, I myself am good-fortune, henceforth I whimper no more, postpone no more, need nothing."[44]

"Aye, I agree George. A person is responsible for their own good fortune in life." Dehlia confided. But I think I do detect a slight whimper from you my good man!" she laughed.

"Oh the bonny lass is correct! But no more! Farewell self-

---

[44] *Song of the Open Road*, Walt Whitman

doubt and depreciation! I will stop at nothing until my good-fortune is collected in spades! Forward march toward the open road!" he emoted.

George and Dehlia, safely ensconced within the warm sleigh, swept down the road alongside the heavily forested and newly named Forest Park. George began to aptly describe the scenery vividly swirling past them.

"Boating is a very popular sport in the summer here Dehlia, and we certainly will take a boat ride in the spring, I promise you that, but what I really wanted to show you is the wonderful statue of Edward Bates. Look! See it proudly standing in the park? It was erected in 1876, long before you crossed the Atlantic."

"Who was this Mr. Bates, George? Why are you showing me his statue?"

When they pulled the sleigh up alongside the monument and stopped, George's face became serious as he said, "Edward Bates was the Attorney General under our great President, Abraham Lincoln. Mr. Bates was a very prominent attorney and judge here in St. Louis. Perhaps you have heard about our Civil War? It was a conflict between political factions over the freedoms our Constitution was written to insure, that all men are entitled to their freedom from tyranny and grief, much like your Irish Rebellion, only the people in question were called slaves, not poor Irish farmers, as in your case. Well, Mr. Bates willingly and legally assisted freedom suits brought by the poor and destitute slaves. He was a brave man and stood up for what he believed in, just like you Dehlia. In his honor, this statue was the very first one installed in the park."

"Aye George. We too had a brave hero who sought to unite the groups of the Protestants, Catholic and Dissenters in the rectification of their grievances by breaking the link with England."[45] His name was Wolfe Tone." Dehlia had surprised herself by declaring this statement and nervously glanced at George to see if he had taken offense.

George replied knowledgably, "Of course, the year 1798 was the most tragic event in Irish History between the Jacobite Wars and the Great Famine."[46] I have studied your Irish and my English history quite well but there seems to be a slight disconnect between the two streams of thought." He added. "At least, I suppose, your young Michael did not have to suffer pitch capping!"

"Pitch capping? Whatever is that? Dehlia asked, taken aback by George's knowledge of the Irish Rebellion.

"Well, I'm not too proud of my English forebears and some of their actions. A canvas crown was placed on the head of an insurgent, much like your man Wolfe Tone, or an alleged insurgent, and boiling tar was poured into the canvas surround. After this had had time to set, the cap was torn off, taking with it much of the "croppy's scalp."

Dehlia gasped with the thought of such a dastardly deed!

"I know," George added, that was a terribly cruel thing to do to another person but sometimes as human beings, we often let our emotions and righteous indignations run amuck

[45] McCullough, David Willis, *War of the Irish Kings*, Three Rivers Press, NY
[46] Coogan, Tim Pat, *The Famine Plot: England's Role in Irelands Greatest Tragedy*, Palgrave MacMillan, N.Y., 2012

so we forget to be kind. At least when your Wolfe Tone was captured he cheated the hangman by committing suicide, a coward's way out!"

"You don't know how it feels to be oppressed George!" she yelled back. "You can't fathom how each pitiful day turns and twists into yet another dawn of despair! Young men like Michael had no choice but to fight for the freedom to work and keep their hard earned money for themselves and their families! I know now that Michael loved his "cause" more than he loved me but at least he tried to do something to right the wrongs our countrymen had pushed upon them by the likes of the English!"

"I'm sorry Dehlia, I didn't mean to criticize. I suppose I will never understand the turmoil you have experienced but I do know that I have loved you from the moment I laid eyes on you." George quietly stated. "I know you cannot make up your mind to let yourself go and love again. I realize your emotions are paralyzed by the torment of loving and losing someone as valiant as Michael, and I know I can't compete with his exemplary vision, but my darling, despite our different cultures, my heart urges me on and my mind is made up. You can rest assured, I will not change mine!"

Taken aback by George's profession of admiration, Dehlia rode on in hushed dismay, undecided in how to respond to his admission of lofty affection.

As George quietly but expertly guided the sleigh down Skinker Avenue and onto Lindell Boulevard, he broke the silence and said, "Look up ahead Dehlia. You will be amazed at the marvelous homes wealthy families have built here." She stared in awe at the huge buildings lining the wide street called Lindell. The stately homes all had broad lawns and overhanging trees. She noticed they were constructed of brown stone and white granite, expensive building materials to say the least!

"How many families live in one of these mansions, George?" she asked. "They are so grand, like the mansions in New York, but with such large spaces in the front of the homes for plants and wooden structures." George laughed again and said,

"Oh they are grand homes indeed but only one family lives in each of these Dehlia."

"No, surely not!" she exclaimed.

"This Lindell Boulevard is becoming one of St. Louis' fashionable thoroughfares. The houses have been built by some of the most prominent citizens of the town. In fact, an architect by the name of James P. Jamieson, designed a magnificent mansion for the daughter of James Eads, you know, the famed bridge builder? Mr. Fox, who photographs the wealthy inhabitants, says these houses contain as many as sixteen rooms. He has described grand staircases and oversized halls. There are paneled living rooms, bedrooms with fireplaces and marble bathrooms, all maintained by servants, who live in their own quarters within the house."[47]

"Where are their half-doors, George?"

"What? What are half-doors, Dehlia? These wealthy people have doors that go all the way up to the casing, you

---

[47] History of St. Louis Neighborhoods, *stlouis-mo.gov*

know, so they can admit guests without bending over!" George chuckled at the thought of tall gentlemen attempting to duck low in order to enter a home.

Her face burning with embarrassment, Dehlia stammered. "Why, half-doors in Ireland are lucky, don't you know? We believe they bring good luck, especially when painted red! They ward off evil spirits and ghosts!"

Feeling foolish, she continued to explain. "The half doors in each cottage help to contain the wee children inside and safe from harm. They keep the beasts from entering and making a dirty mess as well!"

"Oh sweet Dehlia! You are a delight to behold! Do you really believe in ghosts?"

"Aye George, sometimes I do, but besides gossiping to the neighbors and shouting to the bairns that supper is ready, I suppose the half door, to me, symbolizes a barrier of sorts. An entry way that lets the light and good in while keeping the bad at bay."

"Yes, I do see indeed! I suppose a comparison could be made too, such as when a person has a choice in life to make, a traveling on a forked road, so to speak. To either let the errant and evil thoughts corrupt their minds or keep their consciousness elevated and lifted up, sort of similar to the top of the half door, right Dehlia?"

"Yes, my maith'er would certainly agree with you George. Our cottages were often damp and musty and the upper part of the door, standing wide open, let the fresh breezes in and the stale odors out!"

Gazing at the magnificent homes lining the wide street,

George smiled and said, "I promise you Dehlia, someday I will own a home as grand as these and perhaps," winking at her, "I might even install a red half door in the front! I would like to paint elegant murals on the walls. In fact, I want to paint the clear blue sky we view now and white fluffy clouds scattered all over it, on my dining room ceiling. I want to always remember this beautiful, wonderful day!"

"Aye, and perhaps you could add in a charming bird or two, swooping over and through your sky?"

"Right you are! It would be Heaven on Earth!" he joyously added.

The next week, George had another surprise in store for Dehlia. When he picked her up, they started walking, hand in hand, toward the landing on the Mississippi where Dehlia had embarked from the steamboat that had brought her to the bustling town of St. Louis.

"I have a treat in store for you today, Dehlia." George winked and said cheerfully. "I have done a little research and feel fairly certain you will agree with the treasure I am about to show you."

What does he mean, a "treasure?" Dehlia thought to herself. I don't need more flowers to show he loves me nor promises to build me huge mansions in the sky. However, George is certainly fascinating and kind. It is a wonderful feeling when someone cares more for you than they care for themselves.

When they arrived down at the riverfront Dehlia noticed she was standing right in front of a beautiful cathedral.

"This is the Basilica of St. Louis, King of France. St.

Louisians also call it the Old Cathedral. It's the oldest cathedral west of the Mississippi River and constructed of native limestone and sandstone!" George exclaimed.

"Oh my, it is breathtakingly beautiful! I saw it when I passed by with Annie and Frank so many months ago, and it reminded me of the churches in Ireland. Thank you for bringing me here."

"You are welcome, but that is not entirely why I brought you here Dehlia. Even though I was raised Presbyterian and not Catholic, like you, I nevertheless have found this old cathedral enchanting. You see, a long time ago, in about 1764, the founders of St. Louis, Pierre Laclede and Auguste Chouteau, loyal Frenchmen to the core, set aside a tract of land to construct a cemetery, a church and also homes."

"Did they build the church as it looks today?" Dehlia questioned.

"No, in fact, the first church was made all of logs. They named it after it's' patron saint, St. Louis IX, King of France. What I find interesting is this. Louis was only twelve when he was crowned King and at his coronation, he was bound by an oath to behave as God's anointed and father of his people. Now, other kings had been commanded to do the same but had also wrecked wars and violence during their reigns. This young King interpreted his kingly duties in the light of faith and strove to bring peace and justice to France."[48]

"Hah," Dehlia exclaimed. "You mean the king actually chose peace over strife? That is unheard of among most men!"

---

[48] *oldcathedralstl.org*

"It's true! King Louis was devoted to his people. He visited the sick and even went to the leprosy colonies to care for them. Everyday Louis invited thirteen special guests from among the poor to eat with him. He also was known to serve meals to large numbers of poor near his palace."

"Well it is no wonder Pierre Laclede honored him so. What an unselfish monarch! When did the log cabin church become one carved out of magnificent stone?" Dehlia asked.

"I think it was about 1830 or so before it was rebuilt. Did you know that many of the Indians, like the Nez Perce tribe, would travel here to learn of the Christian faith? They would boat down the river from the mountains in the west to see for themselves. But Dehlia, the outside of the cathedral is not all I wanted to show you. Let's go inside. I have a couple of paintings to show you."

When Dehlia entered the church doors she felt in awe of the opulence and grandeur before her. She could only stare wide-eyed at the beauty of the large clear-glass windows, the pristine white columns and walls with gilded gold moldings. As the young couple respectfully entered the sanctuary, George admonished Dehlia.

"Turn around and look behind you! See this amazing portrait of the young St. Louis IX, on his coronation night? Aren't the colors of the robes brilliant? What courage this king had and at such an early age! His strong character reminds me of you, Dehlia! And just as you did in Ireland, he strove to help the poor and destitute in France. What a legacy! However, the portrait I really wanted you to view is the one hanging over the altar."

Dehlia swirled around and gazed upon the large painting of Jesus hanging over the altar. "It is absolutely amazing and so life-like. The skin looks so realistic I think I could actually reach out and pinch it!" Dehlia exclaimed. "And look at the face of Jesus! I don't believe I ever saw anything as poignant in Mrs. Vanderbilt's collection in New York. I recognize Christ on the cross, but who was the artist who painted it?"

"Velazquez. Diego Velazquez, a Spanish painter from Madrid, about 1630 or 32."

"It's so large and commanding, George. Did the church commission it when they rebuilt the cathedral from a tiny log church?"

"I believe so, but I am not really sure. I do know that this is not the original painting but a magnificent copy! Nevertheless, I come here often to gaze at the beautiful translucent colors Velazquez used for the skin of Christ. I have learned that the pigments of yellow, red and blue mixed with some white create a flesh tone but just look at the undertones of blues and greens! The skin fairly glows from within! I am constantly examining the canvas for clues to his genius. I often wonder how a human being could re-create reality with such passion and god-like skill. I am in awe of his creativity! I feel like such an amateur artist in the masters' presence. I wonder if I will ever be able to create a portrait as glorious as this!"

When George glanced back down at Dehlia, he saw salty tears well up in her eyes and start to flow down her pink cheeks.

"Thank you for taking the time to share your heart with

me. It has been such a long time since someone described their passion to me. It did my soul good to hear you cry out with your emotions. I trust God will fulfill your desire to become the artist you wish to be. You have an open-mind and a kind heart. Those are virtues that don't go unnoticed by Him."

In a quiet and sacred moment George and Dehlia reverently lit candles in the cathedral for their families, experiencing together the joy as well as the grief that arrives with love.

"The Crucifixion" by Diego Rodriquez Velaquez, ca. 1632 (oldcathedralstl.org)

I am so lucky to be spending time with this compassionate soul, Dehlia considered.

She began to realize the dramatic new thread of her existence now included a gentle and resilient man, ever thoughtful, ever consistent and kind. Though George embodied all of these attributes, he was careful not to push

Dehlia further into any sort of commitment of the heart. He was mature enough to know that time and sincere, candid conversations would build up her confidence in him. He was patient and willing to wait for the reward of that.

One fine spring day, in early May, while sitting for a while on Frank and Annie's' front stoop, she and George were discussing her trials from Castle Garden.

"I can't believe I was such a hair-brained, naïve little ninny, George! Why, I was absolutely asking for bad luck to fool me!"

"I have read newspaper accounts that Castle Garden was so corrupt and overrun with felons that the government has now built a new immigration center they call Ellis Island." George remarked.

"Aye, George, that was a bad place, indeed! Remember how I told you I had to sell my *mai'thers'* silver cross for money after I was robbed."

"Yes, I do remember my Darling." George began to fumble around in his suit pocket. After a few awkward seconds, he located the source of his agitation and reverently pulled out a small white box, tied up with a shiny blue bow.

Standing up and bowing low, he proudly said, "Allow me to present you with this small token of my esteem."

Dehlia gasped as she gingerly opened the tiny box and hesitantly lifted out a small gold ring with a heart and crown on it.

"Oh my! George, I don't know what to say! You know I'm not ready to become engaged, or tender my life to anyone yet!" Babbling on, if only for the chance to stall for time, she squeaked out, "Why, suffragettes in America are now asking for "the vote" as well as equal property rights in marriage! I want to adopt this country and help to spread the mantra of equal rights for women! I admire the courage it takes for women to stand on their own feet, so to speak, so they won't have to rely on a husband to support them, like I expected Michael to take care of me! I have plans to succeed in my own future business venture! I'm slowly learning what choices I have and forge my individual path in life! I can't offer my heart to someone else until I have mended, become my own person and learned to love myself as well." Dehlia paused and looked fondly at George while having a difficult time making up her mind how best to describe her feelings. She took the time to notice George simply smiling and gazing at her with those same, tender eyes she noticed when she first met him at the photographer's studio, so many months ago. Taking a deep breath she quietly but firmly stated, "Although you are the kindest and most thoughtful man I have ever known, you must know I am not ready for the commitment of marriage. I won't change my mind!"

"I do know that Dehlia." George kindly said, "This is not entirely an engagement ring, although I wouldn't mind a bit if that is what you wished it to be but simply one to replace the lost silver cross your mam gave you. I know it pains you to have lost it. You see here, this is a Claddagh cross ring, one that I understand mothers hand down to their beloved daughters."

"Yes, I see that George, but if you are not asking me to marry you, why are you giving this to me?"

"I thought you should begin new traditions now and not stay stuck in the past with sadness and regrets. You can wear this ring until you have a daughter old enough to give it to, and," he laughed, as if he knew a secret, "a girl as independent as you! Look at the carvings. The jeweler said the two hands holding the crowned heart is the symbol to represent love, faith and eternity."

"Aye, and in Ireland the crowned heart also represents God the Father. The two charming hands signify Jesus and the Holy Spirit." She added.

"And, I shall say to you my Darling, with these hands, I give you my heart and crown it with love." George whispered quietly, while averting his eyes. "You must know by now that I have loved you from the moment we met but I have been paralyzed with the thought that I might disappoint you. I feel a heavy burden that I am in competition with your Michael. At times I can't make up my mind to pursue you or allow you the space to breathe."

"Aye, George, I think I know I still carry an ache in my heart for Michael and I feel the loss of him often, especially in my dreams. I am afraid of the pain of betrayal and heartache that devoted love sometimes claims. I can't bring myself to trust another man again but, but thank you, from the bottom of my heart! She stammered. I have learned a thing or two from you and I promise I will adopt a new attitude. You have taught me to accept the future with my arms wide open and gather all the happiness Life can bestow on me! I am grateful for your kindness and patience and, who knows? Perhaps someday, when I am made whole, I will be able to return your affection, in kind." George glanced back up and caught his breath. Hope began to swell in his breast.

Seeing the ardent love on his face, Dehlia gently continued, "I may very well be making the wrong decision and I do fear I will regret it in the future but nevertheless, I need more time to mend my frayed heart. I cannot truly be yours when my heart is still in tattered pieces. It may take years, but I assure you Mr. Watts, I will survive this! I will! You have been a true friend and I'll always cherish the promise of a happier future with you, should I decide to pursue it."

"Well, remember Love," George tenderly continued, "the hard things in life make you stronger, not weaker. They may not make you happier but I guarantee, they will demand that you learn of either your inner strength or your pitiful frailty. Hard lessons exact a price! They either make you more equipped to persevere or become bitter from the disappointments. You have to choose."

With that, George knew what he must do. Courageously smiling and with his blue eyes twinkling, he arose from stoop, where they were comfortably sitting. He gently tipped his hat to Dehlia and slowly started walking away. Turning around, he stopped, considered his words for a moment, then took the time to caution her once more.

"Yes Dehlia, decide. The future or the past! Only one can be the Master."

"Aye George," She thoughtfully confessed. "I feel as though I am crossing, once more, through a half-door. Only this time, I must choose between faithfully allowing in the light or fearlessly letting out the darkness. However, I don't think I am capable of doing both chores at the same time."

Smiling at the pondering face before him, George divulged, "My father Jeremiah is wise as well as a man of the cloth. He has a favorite passage from the Bible. I have often heard him quote it to his congregation. He tells them this story."

"Moses was commanded by the Lord to make an agreement with the Israelites in Moab. Moses told the Israelites, "Today I ask heaven and earth to be witnesses. I am offering you life or death, blessings or curses. Now, I say, choose life! Then you and your children may live. To choose life is to love the Lord your God, obey him, and stay close to him. He is your life, and he will let you live many years in the land, the land he promised to give your ancestors."[49]

George continued, "So, Dehlia, gather up onto your lap the tattered quilt blocks that portray your life and those of your ancestors. Examine each and every square for what it represents. Turn them over and examine the backs. Can't you just imagine the tangled mess of threads? Yet, when you turn the pieces over, the fronts become glorious masterpieces of beauty!

My dear, bind up all those sorrows you hold within your heart. Fuse the woes and tribulations together until you feel they cannot harm you. Weave the sadness you once embraced into a forgiven nest of the past. Then, piece by piece, begin to splice and stitch another quilt, a better one, embroidered with

---

[49] Bible, Deuteronomy 30:19, Max Lucado NIV

peace and contentment. When you are ready, God willing, choose that!"

Dehlia Fleming - March 17, 1868 – August 20, 1942

Postscript

"On May 22, 1998, more than two million people across Ireland voted for the Good Friday Agreement, an international Agreement which was the collective product of inclusive negotiations and a compromise between political opponents. While the Agreement itself does not resolve the causes of conflict, it does, if implemented, set out a political and institutional framework within which many of the causes of conflict can be addressed."[50]

"The Agreement affirmed a commitment to "the mutual respect, the civil rights and the religious liberties of everyone in the community". The multi-party agreement recognized "the importance of respect, understanding and tolerance in relation to linguistic diversity", especially in relation to the *Irish language*, *Ulster Scots*, and the languages of Northern Ireland's ethnic minorities, "all of which are part of the cultural wealth of the island of Ireland."

The Voice by Celtic Woman on a New Journey
Brendan Graham

I am the voice of the past that will always be
Filled with my sorrow and blood in my fields
I am the voice of the future, bring me your peace.
Bring me your peace, and my wounds, they will heal.

---

[50] *sinnfein.ie/good-friday-agreement*

About the Author

My name is Rusty Watson and I currently live in Mt. Vernon, IL. I grew up in St. Louis, Missouri, among a large group of very talented family members who worked and created fine art, sang opera, played musical instruments and read novels with a passion. After obtaining my fine art degree from Washington University, I had an exciting career as a fashion designer but when the workday was over, I usually had my "head in a book." My desire to learn permitted me to go back to college and obtain my teaching degree. I hope I have instilled that same desire for knowledge in the hearts and minds of the hundreds of Kindergarten and Art students I have taught through the years. I believe this cognizance has manifested itself in my desire to research and write about the past generations who have nurtured us and set examples for our behaviors. History is my interest but the retelling of it within the structure of a personal story is my passion. After all, how can we face the future without learning from the past?

Although I am currently teaching art and free lancing as a children's' book illustrator, this is my second written novel. Creating words on a page is similar to creating artistic marks on a canvas. I feel blessed to be able to make my family proud.

Recent Releases from
Casa de Snapdragon

The Wound Dresser
Jack Coulehan
ISBN: 978-1-937240-73-8
Genre: Poetry

Jack Coulehan's sixth collection of poems explores the mysterious tension between tenderness and steadiness in medical practice. Coulehan seeks to emulate the tender care shown by Walt Whitman as he comforted wounded Civil War soldiers. With directness, passion, and often humor, these poems evoke an ethic of compassionate solidarity — between patient and doctor, person and family, the individual and the human community. Robert Pinsky, Poet Laureate of the United States from 1997 to 2000, selected *The Wound Dresser* as a finalist for the 2016 Dorset Poetry Prize.

Grabbing the Apple
An Anthology of New York Poets
Edited by Terri Muuss and MJ Tenerelli
ISBN: 978-1-937240-70-7
Genre: Poetry

In this beautiful collection of over 40 New York women poets, the strength, vitality and unique voices of women emerge. Energy, savvy, wisdom and power emanate from these poems, both individually and as a collection. The women whose work has been anthologized in this collection are as brave as Eve. Not content to have their stories told for them, these poets grab the apple with both hands and tell it themselves. *Grabbing the Apple* is a powerful resource for any reader or student who wants to explore an in-depth selection of work from some of New York's finest and strongest women poets.

A Witches' Garden
Trish Breedlove
ISBN: 978-1-937240-68-4
Genre: Gardening

From the very basics of where to place your garden, how big should it be, what plants should you include all the way down to how to use the bounty of your harvest, Trish leaves no stone unturned and the only questions that remain are; When will you start your own and What are you waiting for?

Take Any Ship That Sails
Michele Heeney
ISBN: 978-1-937240-67-7
Genre: Poetry

This 5th book of Michele's spans 45 years of writing poems and thousands of miles of geography. It is a selection of poems from when Michele was in her teens in Pennsylvania to recent poems inspired by the beautiful mountains and Mesas of New Mexico. There are poems from Monterey and Marin counties, California. From times spent writing at Esalenin Big Sur. A few are from her time in Hawaii. They cover nature, love, art, and personal growth. There are some of free verse and classical form. Her favorite poets are many, including the sufi poets Rumi and Hafiz, the English and Irish poets, including Seamus Heaney. If you love poetry, this is a book for you.

Geographic
A Memoir of Time and Space
Miriam Sagan
ISBN: 978-1-937240-62-2
Genre: Biographies & Autobiographies, Personal Memoirs

Miriam Sagan has written a book that tells in poetic beauty the often difficult and frequently uplifting history of her own life and challenges as she tumbles through the mixture of events that helped contribute to the writer that she is today.

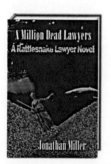

A Million Dead Lawyers
A Rattlesnake Lawyer Novel
Jonathan Miller
ISBN: 978-1-937240-65-3
Genre: Sci-Fi, Legal Thrillers

"What do you call a thousand dead lawyers at the bottom of the sea?" "A good start." Sam Marlow, a street-front lawyer from present day Albuquerque, suddenly finds himself in the year 2112. There are no attorneys and all verdicts are rendered by computer. He has to handle the first actual jury trial in nearly a hundred years. The governor's son is accused of killing his wife, and the whole system lies in the balance. Needless to say, nothing is what it seems and yet some people seem strangely familiar. With the help of a beautiful wannabe lawyer, he's soon able to get started in this brave new legal world, even though the authorities are against them. But is the Albuquerque of the future ready for a rattlesnake lawyer?